PUPPY PATROL ™

SHERLOCK'S HOME

JENNY DALE

Illustrations by Mick Reid
Cover illustration by Michael Rowe

AN
APPLE
PAPERBACK

SCHOLASTIC INC.
New York Toronto London Auckland Sydney
Mexico City New Delhi Hong Kong Buenos Aires

SPECIAL THANKS TO LORNA READ

No part of this publication may be reproduced, in whole or in part, or stored in a retrieval system, or transmitted in any form or by any means, electronic, mechanical, photocopying, recording, or otherwise, without written permission of the publisher. For information regarding permission, please write to Macmillan Publishers Ltd., 20 New Wharf Rd., London N1 9RR Basingstoke and Oxford.

ISBN 0-439-29675-7

12 11 10 9 8 7   6 7 8/0

Printed in the U.S.A.   40
First printing, March 2003

CHAPTER ONE

"Careful, Dad!" Neil Parker clutched the pet carrier on his knee firmly, steadying it as the King Street Kennels Range Rover hit a flooded pothole in the road.

"I'm going to speak to Councilman Jepson about the state of this road," Bob Parker complained angrily. Neil's father jerked the steering wheel to steady the vehicle and keep it firmly under control as they crawled through the darkness. "Imagine if I'd been driving any faster! That carrier might have hit the windshield!"

"I hope Pepé's all right," said Neil worriedly. It was too dark a night to see the tiny occupant inside the carrier, but the little short-haired Chihuahua was very quiet. Neil didn't know if this was a good sign or not.

Dogs were the most important things in Neil's life. His parents ran King Street Kennels and rescue center near the small country town of Compton. He'd become very interested in dogs' health problems and illnesses since his own dog, Sam, a superb black-and-white Border collie, had developed a heart condition.

Pepé, one of their many current boarding dogs, had looked seriously ill less than half an hour ago when Neil had found him in his pen twitching and shaking. Now Neil was impatient to get him to the vet as fast as possible. That was, if the driving sleet and battering wind would allow them to get to Mike Turner's clinic at all. There was so much icy slush blowing onto the windshield that the wipers were barely able to do their job.

The gale gathered strength as it blew across the open country fields. A blast of wind howled outside and Neil felt the vehicle lurch. Bob held the wheel steady.

Suddenly, like a flash of lightning, a powerful beam of light lit up the inside of the car.

Dazzled, Neil turned his head away from the bright light.

"What the . . . ?" Bob stamped his foot on the brakes.

The tires of the Range Rover screeched on the slippery road's surface and the heavy vehicle skidded to the right.

Neil flung both arms around the pet carrier on his lap and held on tight as the Range Rover hit the shoulder, lurched upward, and then came to a stop with a jolt, leaving two wheels planted firmly halfway up the grassy slope.

"What on earth was that?" Bob exclaimed in a shocked tone. "I wasn't sure if it was another vehicle coming straight for us or not. Sorry, Neil. Are you and Pepé OK?"

"Yes, don't worry." Neil looked down at the carrier. "I didn't drop him." Gathering his wits, Neil strained to see out of the murky windshield. The wipers were still struggling to clear the view as the car engine hummed eerily in the darkness. "Look, it's the police! I wonder what's going on?"

The beam of light had come from the powerful flashlight carried by a police officer. Farther along the road, Neil saw him running out of the driveway of a large, isolated house. The flashlight beam picked out the blurred shape of a speeding dog that was hurtling ahead of the officer down the country road.

"It looks like Jasper!" Neil exclaimed.

"Then that must be Sergeant Moorhead," Bob replied. Jasper was Compton's talented and popular police dog. The long-serving six-year-old German shepherd and the local sergeant he lived with were inseparable.

As Neil rolled down his window and craned his head outside to get a better look, he could hear the dog's excited barks as he ran.

"Chase, Jasper!" Sergeant Moorhead shouted urgently, before speaking rapidly into his radio.

At first, Neil couldn't see the person the police dog was supposed to be chasing. Then the wavering flashlight caught a shadowy figure running along the hedge by the road. In the distance, a second beam of light appeared and another officer could be seen racing toward the scene from the opposite direction.

"Let's get out and help!" Neil said eagerly.

His father quickly put a restraining hand on his arm. "No, Neil. For all we know, that man could be armed," he hissed. "We'd better leave chasing and catching criminals to the police. We could lend a light to things, though . . ."

Bob flicked on their high beams. He rolled the Range Rover down off the shoulder and began inching forward very slowly toward the scene of the action.

Now the escaping man could be seen more clearly. He was heading for a car parked against the gate to a field. Both Sergeant Moorhead and his partner were having difficulty staying on their feet on the icy road and, before either officer could apprehend him, the man reached his car and yanked open the driver's door.

But he hadn't reckoned with the speed of four legs!

Jasper was faster and soon caught him. With an enormous bound, the dog's jaws gripped the sleeve of the man's jacket. The big German shepherd growled menacingly and pulled hard, preventing the man from climbing into the car.

Neil watched openmouthed as the struggle between man and beast continued.

The powerful, muscular dog used all his strength to tug, his paws scraping for traction on the slushy road, while the man struck out desperately with both feet and his free hand.

Just when it seemed that Jasper was winning and would manage to hold on until one of the officers reached him, the sleeve tore off the man's jacket. Finding himself free at last, he hurled himself into his car.

Jasper jumped up after him.

Then came a sound that made Neil feel momentarily sick — the simultaneous slam of a car door and agonized shriek of the dog whose paw had been trapped and crushed in it.

As Neil watched, transfixed with horror, the car door opened and Jasper, yelping in pain, fell onto the road. Then everything seemed to happen at nightmare speed. The door slammed again and the car engine roared to life, shooting forward toward the Range Rover.

Jasper disappeared underneath the wheels.

"Nooooo!" screamed Neil.

The driver must have felt the bump as he ran over the injured dog, but he didn't stop.

Before Neil could leap out to Jasper's aid, a motorcycle roared past from behind, and a gust of wind rustled Neil's hair. It swerved violently to get out of the path of the car as it hurtled toward them, only just missing the dark shape that was lying so still on the gleaming wet road. It was a miracle that the motorcycle wasn't hit, too. The rider stopped for a moment, appeared to quickly take in what was going on around him, then flung his machine around and sped off again in pursuit of the disappearing car. The bike whizzed past Neil's ear for a second time.

Neil instinctively thrust the pet carrier onto his dad's lap and leaped from the Range Rover, ignoring Bob's cries to come back at once. Freezing sleet lashed his face and crept down the neck of his jacket as he neared the injured dog.

Sergeant Moorhead was already bending by the dog's side, shining the flashlight over him. The second officer was nowhere to be seen.

"Is he . . ." gasped Neil, "is he OK?"

"The car went right over him," the sergeant said with a catch in his voice. The policeman seemed reluctant to touch him, as if he was scared that he would hurt the dog further.

Neil felt a lump form in his throat. *How could anybody be so cruel?* In the light from the flashlight and the Range Rover's headlights, Neil could see dark blood oozing from Jasper's nose and mouth. He knew it didn't look good. The police dog's crushed paw was also bleeding badly.

The noise of another car engine made Neil look up for a second, and he saw a police car drive after the fleeing assailant and motorcycle.

Then Bob crouched down and joined them. Neil and the sergeant shuffled along to make room for him. Bob quickly felt for a pulse in the fur on the dog's neck. "He's still alive. Let's get him straight to the clinic."

"I'll come with you," said the sergeant with relief in his voice.

"We'll need to move him as little as possible," said Bob urgently. "He may have back injuries. Neil?"

"Yes, Dad?"

"Call Mike and tell him we've now got *two* patients for him." He took his cell phone out of his pocket and handed it over. "Tell him what's happened so that he's prepared. This is an emergency."

"Thanks, Bob," said the sergeant. He tentatively reached out his hand and began stroking the dog's head gently.

Neil stood up and looked around. He could still barely believe what was happening. He stabbed a finger in the direction that the car and the motorcycle had driven off. "But . . . won't that man be getting away?"

The police sergeant remained calm. "Constable Grey will follow him. My place is here. I need to . . . look after Jasper."

Neil punched out Mike's number on the phone and made the call for help.

Oblivious to the sleeting rain, Bob took off his jacket and laid it on the road, waterproof side down. Then, very gently, working together, he and Sergeant Moorhead carefully slid the heavy body of the unconscious German shepherd onto the jacket. Holding it taut between them, they carried it toward the Range Rover. Neil finished the call and pocketed the phone, then rushed to open the rear door to the dog cage.

"I'll get in with him to keep him from being thrown around," the sergeant insisted.

High-pitched yaps were coming from the abandoned Pepé.

Neil felt a pang of guilt. In the heat of the moment, Neil had almost forgotten about him. Bob spoke soothingly to the tiny dog through the mesh of the carrier. The dog looked nervous and his shiny, short, pointed muzzle glistened in the shadows of the carrier. Bob handed it to Neil to hold as he got into the driver's seat and pulled the door closed. Neil buckled himself in and, at last, they were on their way again toward Compton.

Neil suspected that the sergeant probably didn't want to talk about the assault on Jasper, but he was desperate to make sense of the drama that had just happened. He couldn't resist asking the questions that were burning in his mind. "Sergeant Moorhead, I'm sorry about Jasper. But who was that man? Why were you at the house?"

"Neil!" said Bob angrily.

"No, it's OK, Bob." The sergeant continued stroking Jasper as he spoke. "We had an anonymous tip that the house was going to be burglarized tonight. It's the weekend home for a city businessman, who we know owns a lot of very valuable antique jewelry."

The sergeant's account was interrupted when Jasper made a sickening, throaty, choking noise.

Neil stiffened. "Hang in there, boy," he sighed. "We'll be there soon."

"Yes, we're almost there," said Bob.

The policeman nodded, then continued. "Anyway, we thought we'd stake the place out and catch him red-handed. Trouble was, he arrived before us and was already in there taking what he was after. When we saw a flashlight moving around inside, we moved in. He must have heard us and tried to make a run for it." The sergeant inhaled deeply. "That's when you arrived, I think. And you saw what happened to Jasper . . ." His voice trailed off.

"We're here!" announced Neil quickly, hoping to lessen the sergeant's grief.

As they pulled up on the gravel driveway outside the veterinary clinic, Neil saw Mike Turner standing in the doorway, watching for them. He rushed toward them. *We've made it,* Neil thought. Now Jasper and Pepé could get the medical attention they both desperately needed.

Bob yanked open the rear car door and Mike climbed in beside the sergeant. Neil leaned back to watch. The vet bent over Jasper, felt for a pulse, tentatively listened for a heartbeat, then turned to the three concerned faces that stared so hopefully at him.

"I'm sorry," he said, shaking his head, "it's too late."

"No, Mike!" cried Neil. "He was breathing a minute ago. Check him again."

Sergeant Moorhead lowered his head.

Bob rested his hand on the policeman's shoulder.

"Neil," the vet persisted, "there's nothing I can do. I'm afraid he's gone. Jasper is dead."

CHAPTER TWO

For the rest of that tragic evening, Neil felt like a zombie. He was numb with grief for poor Jasper and Sergeant Moorhead. He knew he would *never* forget the stricken look on the sergeant's face when Mike Turner told him that the police dog was dead.

"You go on inside with Pepé, Neil," said Bob Parker. "We'll take care of this."

Neil sat alone in the clinic with the carrier on his knee. Inside it, Pepé seemed to have become very lively. He was pawing at the wire front, yapping. If he could have scratched or wriggled his way out, he certainly would have.

When Neil poked his fingers through the wire and ran them along his smooth, glossy coat, Pepé shifted around and his warm tongue licked them, making Neil feel a little better.

Eventually, Mike and Bob reappeared.

"The sergeant's been picked up and taken back to the station," said Bob. "Jasper's going to stay here tonight." He ran a hand over his dripping hair and beard. "I feel as if I've been in a shower with all my clothes on," he said. "And look at you!"

Neil suddenly realized how wet he was. He was cold to the bone and his socks and shoes were soaked through.

"You'd better get home quickly or you'll catch pneumonia," Mike said. "Let me just take a look at this little fellow here. What did you say his symptoms were when you found him?"

Despite his grief for Jasper, Neil tried to focus on Pepé's plight. "He looked as if he was having a seizure," he explained. "He was trembling all over and his mouth was frothing. And he was coughing and wheezing, too. I was really worried about him. I can't understand how he could have recovered so quickly. He seems so much better now."

Neil remained anxious as Mike gently lifted the tiny dog out of the carrier and placed him on a large examining table.

"There doesn't seem to be *anything* the matter with him," the vet said. "His temperature's fine and his heart and breathing are normal." Mike gently touched several different places over the dog's small body. "And he doesn't seem to be in pain anywhere." Looking into Pepé's mouth, he added, "He is salivating slightly, though. See this dribble on his mouth? I think it's best if he stays in overnight for observation. I'll give you a call in the morning with an update."

"So there's no need to worry just yet?" asked Bob.

"No, I don't think so. Chihuahuas can be . . ."

"Yes?" said Neil hurriedly.

"Well, they're great tremblers, you know. They just have to get a little scared or overexcited, and they start to quiver. So don't worry about that," Mike said.

"Come on." Bob put an arm around Neil's shoulders. "Let's get home. Mike's absolutely right. We'll catch something terrible if we don't get out of these wet clothes soon."

"And what have you two been up to?" scolded Carole Parker as her husband and son dripped their way into the front hall of their house back at King Street. "You look terrible!"

Sam, the Border collie, roused himself from a slumber by the living room fire and padded up to Neil, wagging his tail. Jake, Sam's young son, dived out from behind the sofa and curled himself around Neil's wet legs. Jake was always full of energy — no matter what the hour or situation.

Neil raised a smile and gave the puppy a pat on the side, then ordered him to sit. He crouched down and hugged Sam, grateful for his faithful affection. Over his head he was aware of Bob and Carole talking about Jasper's fatal accident.

Carole was devastated by the news. "Hot showers right now for the both of you," she ordered in a choked voice. "I'll make some hot chocolate to warm you up."

Bob and Neil were soon back downstairs again, feeling better in body but not in spirit.

Emily, Neil's nine-year-old younger sister, had been upstairs getting ready for bed, but she dashed down again in her slippers and robe when she heard the commotion and joined everybody in the living room.

"How's Pepé?" she asked brightly. "What was it?" Then, noticing the gloomy faces, her expression changed. "Oh, no! It's not serious, is it?" she asked in horror.

Neil struggled to speak. His thoughts flashed back to Jasper's terrible, agonized cries of pain when the car had mangled him earlier that evening.

"Em, I've got some bad news," said Bob sadly. "It's not about Pepé — he's fine, we think."

"It's Jasper . . ." mumbled Neil.

Breakfast the next morning was a solemn affair in the Parker house, especially since there was one more person who still had to be told — Neil and Emily's five-year-old sister, Sarah. She immediately burst into tears and refused to be comforted, even when Jake licked her ankle under the table — something that normally made her shriek and giggle.

Emily put her arm around her. "Come on, Sarah. We're all very sad, but crying can't bring him back. Let's go see what Fudge is up to, shall we?"

But Sarah showed no interest in her pet hamster and even refused her breakfast. Jasper was all she could think of.

Neil had no appetite, either. He hadn't slept well, and it wasn't just because of his horrible experience the previous night. For the last few evenings, they'd all been disturbed by heartrending howls from the rescue center. The culprit was Mickey, a black-and-white mongrel. Everyone was doing their best to make him feel loved and help him settle in, but so far with no success. That night, the howls had bothered Neil more than usual. They made him think about Jasper and the terrible sound he had made when he got trapped in the car door.

"So Compton is without a police dog," Bob said as he munched a piece of toast.

How can Dad eat at a time like this? thought Neil. He pushed his cereal bowl away from the table.

"How about Sergeant Moorhead having a rescue dog?" suggested Emily. "Couldn't the police use one of those?"

Bob shook his head. "I'm afraid not. Police dogs have to be specially trained from when they're puppies. And they don't use just any old breed, either. It's mostly German shepherds."

"No police dog could ever be as good as Jasper was," Neil said wistfully.

Sarah gave a loud sniff. "Will Jasper be buried here, Dad?"

"I think Sergeant Moorhead will have to decide that, sweetheart," said Bob. "He might like to bury Jasper in his own yard."

At that moment, Neil felt a tug under the table as Jake chewed on one of his shoelaces. "Jake, get off!" Despite his low spirits, he reached down and playfully petted Jake's ears. "Time for your walk, I think," he said, grateful for an opportunity for a breath of fresh air.

"Be quick, Neil, or you'll be late for school," said Carole. "And let's all try to cheer up a little, OK? It's stopped raining and, look, the sun's even coming out."

Neil tried to smile, but he knew it was going to take a little while longer before he started laughing and joking again.

After school that afternoon, Neil and Emily lounged around in front of the television. Neil's hand trailed over the side of his armchair and he absentmindedly stroked Jake's smooth head.

"Did you notice anything funny about Kate this morning?" he asked suddenly.

Emily looked up from her dog magazine. Neither of them ever missed visiting the kennel blocks and rescue center before going to school. Kate McGuire, the longest-serving of their two full-time kennel assistants, usually started work at the crack of dawn. Bev had only recently joined them, when the kennel had expanded and a new, larger rescue center had been built. Both of them were invaluable, and the Parkers knew that King Street couldn't operate smoothly without them.

"Yes, I did!" said Emily indignantly. "She walked right past me and didn't even say hello!"

"Same here," said Neil. "She just didn't seem to hear me. It was as if she was miles away."

Emily shrugged. "Maybe she was just very busy."

"Maybe, but it's not like her to be rude," Neil pointed out. "She's normally so friendly."

Then Carole Parker popped her head around the door. "Are you talking about Kate?"

Neil and Emily nodded, and Carole came into the room and perched on the edge of the sofa. "Mmm. Kate asked if she could have a word with me today, actually." Carole paused and bit her lip. "She . . . well, she might be leaving us, I'm afraid."

"No!" Emily cried. "She can't possibly leave us or the dogs." Her face was white with shock.

"What's happened?" asked Neil. His mind was spinning. What would they do without Kate? She'd been with them so long that she was almost part of the family. Her leaving was unthinkable.

"Well," explained Carole, "Terri McCall has been promoted to the local SPCA office, and her old officer's job will be vacant. Kate's been asked to apply for it."

Carole sighed heavily. She looked strained and anxious. Neil gave her a hug. "Don't worry. We'll help, Mom! I could leave school and then I could be with the dogs all day and —"

"Oh, no, you won't!" Carole replied quickly. "It hasn't come to that yet!"

"Maybe she won't get the job," said Emily.

"But she *might*," said Carole miserably. "She's perfect for it, really. We all know that. We just have to accept that Kate won't be around forever, and we have no right to expect her to stay just because it makes our lives easier."

"It'll be impossible to replace her," said Neil.

"I know. I've tried changing her mind — but I haven't had much luck so far. Anyway, I thought you should know the situation."

"Thanks, Mom," said Neil quietly.

"I'd better go. I need to have a word with Kate before she leaves tonight."

Carole went off, leaving Neil staring at his sister, their minds racing.

"I don't know how Kate could even *think* of leaving the dogs!" Neil erupted.

"She can still work with dogs at the SPCA, though. And all kinds of *other* animals, too," Emily said. "Maybe that's what she wants."

"Maybe," said Neil. "But do you think *we* can try? To persuade Kate to stay?"

Emily's face developed one of her familiar fierce expressions that meant she was concentrating really hard. "Of course we can!" she said.

"Then let's go and find her!"

Neil and Emily rushed out into the yard, but before they could reach the office where they thought she might be, Bev appeared with Mickey, the mongrel who'd kept them awake all night.

"Hello, there!" she said cheerfully and, even though they were still shocked and unhappy about Kate, Neil and Emily couldn't help smiling back at her.

Bev was one of those people you liked right away. She was older than Carole, but was so small, wiry, and speedy that at times Neil forgot, and thought she was closer to his own age! In the short time she had been at the kennels, she had thrown everything into her new job. She got along well with Kate, and the dogs loved her — but there was no way she would be able to manage all the work on her own if Kate left.

"It's funny about Pepé, isn't it?" said Bev.

Neil nodded. "Even Mike doesn't have a clue what is wrong."

"Well, your dad brought him back from the clinic this afternoon," said Bev, smiling. "So he's settled in his pen again if you want to go over there and see him. I've just taken Mickey for a long walk, hoping that he'll be too tired to bark tonight."

"Let's hope so!" said Emily.

Bev and Mickey went off in the direction of the kennel and Neil and Emily continued toward the kennel office. As they approached the door, two raised voices drifted out from inside. Both sounded agitated.

"Don't be ridiculous, Kate," they heard their mother say. "You're just as good as Bev. In some ways you're better, because —"

"But I don't *feel* it, Carole!" Kate cut in.

Neil knew that they shouldn't eavesdrop, but neither of them could help it!

"Bev sometimes . . . makes me feel inadequate," continued Kate. "She's a *natural*. She's so good at what she does."

"She's a lot older than you," said Carole.

"I just feel it's time I left. Please don't think I'm not grateful, Carole. You and Bob are *experts* at what you do and you've been marvelous to me, you really have. But I'm fed up with feeling I'm not as good as everybody else. That's why I'd like to try for the SPCA job. I feel I'd have something special to offer."

Neil and Emily listened as the conversation continued, with their mother vainly trying to convince Kate that she was amazingly good at her job, and Kate refusing to believe it.

When they heard their father calling them, they reluctantly dragged themselves away and ran back toward the house.

Bob was in the kitchen making tea. "I've just been on the phone to Sergeant Moorhead," he said.

"What is it?" asked Emily excitedly. "Have they found that horrible man who killed Jasper?"

"Not quite," said Bob. "But they've traced his car. It was stolen from a parking lot in Colshaw yesterday afternoon."

"No sign of the dog murderer, then?" grumbled Neil.

"'Fraid not. But I do have some rather interesting news for you."

"Yes?" asked Neil. He felt as if nothing could interest him after all the drama he'd experienced during the last twenty-four hours.

"It's about the motorcyclist we saw last night. The one who provided the police with the burglar's car registration number."

"What about him?" Neil suddenly felt anxious about what his father might say next. "Who was it?"

"Somebody you know quite well . . ."

"Stop teasing, Dad." Emily laughed. "Tell us who it was."

Bob scratched his beard. "It was Mr. Harding."

Neil's jaw dropped.

Emily sat down at the table with a thud. "Not *the* Mr. Harding? The ex-policeman Neil caught stealing antiques?"

Bob nodded.

"Jessie's owner," Neil croaked. "He's back."

"He sure is," said Bob.

CHAPTER THREE

Neil gazed at his father. "No! I don't believe it," he said in amazement. "I thought he was still in prison!"

"He was let out early on good behavior," said Bob.

The previous year, Neil and his friend Chris from the Meadowbank School had helped put Harding behind bars for his involvement with a gang of antiques robbers. Neil had gone off in search of Harding after he had left his pregnant Airedale-cross dog, Jessie, at King Street Kennels and failed to return for her. He'd found him tied up in a remote cottage, after Harding had double-crossed the gang. Since then, Neil had often wondered what happened to Jessie and her pups. She was one of the best-trained dogs Neil ever met.

"What a blast from the past!" said Emily.

Neil slowly began to get over the initial shock of discovering that Harding was a free man. "I suppose I always felt that Mr. Harding wasn't really cut out to be a criminal," Neil said. Harding had been a police dog trainer before turning to crime. "He was too fond of dogs to be a *really* bad man."

Bob Parker gave a short laugh. "Maybe you've discovered something that psychologists and historians would be fascinated to learn," he told Neil. "If you go to college, you should write something on the world's most evil people, and whether or not they had dogs!"

Emily cleared her throat. "Did Sergeant Moorhead say anything about Jasper?"

Bob's expression turned serious again. "Yes, he says he had a little ceremony for Jasper earlier this evening. He buried him in his yard. He wanted us to know. He was really grateful for our help and support yesterday."

Neil looked down. He didn't want his dad to see how upset he was. He swallowed hard and said, "I wish we'd been there."

"Some things have to be private, Neil. I'm sure you understand," Bob said.

Neil did.

"He says he's going to have to get a new dog very soon, but it's going to be hard for him to get used to working with a different one."

"Yes, there was something special between Sergeant

Moorhead and Jasper — a little like me and Sam," said Neil. "He really did love that German shepherd . . ."

"Will he have the choice of several dogs?" Emily asked.

"There won't be that many to choose from. Lots of dogs that start training prove unsuitable. Only the best make the grade. But I'm sure he could refuse one if he thought it wasn't the right one for him."

"How old are they when they start training?" Neil asked his father.

"A few months, I think. Sergeant Moorhead will know more about it than I do. Why don't you ask him next time you see him?" said Bob.

"I will. I'd like to know how they're trained. Perhaps I could pick up a few tips to pass on to Jake," said Neil.

"Looks like we're in for another busy Saturday," said Carole the following morning as she glanced out the kitchen window. There was a long line of noisy dogs and their owners waiting outside the old rescue center.

"As usual!" said Emily, munching on her breakfast.

The old rescue center had been converted into a walk-in dog clinic and was staffed by Mike Turner every Saturday morning.

"I hope Mike shows up soon," added Neil. "The noise is deafening."

Their chatter was interrupted by the kitchen door

being flung open with a crash and Bev rushing in. "Come quick! Pepé's having another seizure," she said breathlessly.

Neil crossed the yard in record time and got to Pepé's pen ahead of everybody else. He was horrified to see the tiny brown Chihuahua breathing so fast that it seemed as if his lungs would burst. The dog's rasping coughs made his mouth drip with saliva as he crept around the floor of the pen in a trembling circle.

"What is it?" he asked his mother urgently as he hastily unfastened the pen and rushed inside.

"I don't know. I've never seen anything like it," she replied, shaking her head.

Neil picked Pepé up and cradled his shivering form. "I'll look after him while you see if Mike's arrived yet," he said.

"I think I just saw his car," Emily said.

Carole ran off, leaving Neil to comfort the small, heaving body in his arms. Emily looked on worriedly.

A few minutes later, Carole was back with Mike just behind her. He took one look at Pepé and announced, "It looks like an asthma attack. Let me see." He took his stethoscope out of his bag and held it to Pepé's chest. "That's funny . . ."

Handing the stethoscope to Carole, he took Pepé from Neil, looked into the dog's eyes and ears and felt his chest and abdomen. "Does it say anything about asthma in his kennel notes?" he asked.

The owner of every King Street Kennels resident had to fill in a questionnaire detailing their dog's dietary requirements, dates of vaccinations with copies of certificates, and information about any medical conditions the dog might suffer from. After a quick glance at his chart, Carole declared that Pepé's owner had previously given him a clean bill of health.

"Can a dog suddenly start suffering from asthma?" asked Neil.

"Asthma in dogs is a bit like asthma in humans — it can be brought on by stress," Mike informed him. "The symptoms are dribbling, coupled with acute respiratory distress. Has Pepé ever stayed in a kennel before?"

"He's been *here* before," said Carole. "Twice, in fact. And there wasn't anything wrong with him then."

"It can't be that, then. Something else must have caused it. Let's start by giving him an antihistamine injection. That will relieve his breathing problems," Mike said.

Once Pepé had his injection, the little dog's breathing grew a lot calmer.

"Great. Let's have a really good listen to that chest of yours," said Mike. "You really are a tiny thing, aren't you? Can you hold him still for me, Neil?"

Mike listened intently to Pepé's chest. "This is weird," he said. He beckoned Neil closer. "Listen to this. Can you hear any wheezing in his lungs?"

Neil listened. "No, I can't. They sound clear to me," he said, handing the stethoscope back to Mike.

"Can I listen, too?" asked Bev. "You're right," she said, handing back the stethoscope. "He isn't wheezing at all."

"Whatever this little guy has got, then, it's not asthma. No wheeze means no asthma," Mike said. "And an asthma attack doesn't clear up like lightning, which is what happened to Pepé the other night. By the time you brought him in, he seemed fully recovered. There's got to be some other explanation . . ."

"What has he got, then?" Bev asked eagerly.

Mike picked Pepé up and examined him all over. Suddenly, he cried, "Aha!"

"What have you found?" Neil asked him.

"Have a look yourself," Mike said, carefully lifting up one of Pepé's front legs.

Neil looked. Right in the spot where the leg joined the body was an itchy-looking pink patch.

"It's an allergic rash," said Mike. "I'll give you some cream to rub on it. Pepé is allergic to *something* in his environment. The trouble with allergies is that the symptoms don't show until you're in contact with whatever you're allergic to. The whole area of allergies is a pretty mysterious one."

"What on earth can Pepé be allergic to?" Carole wondered despairingly.

"Dust, paint, his bedding . . . it could be one of many things. The only way of finding out for sure is to do tests, but I really need his owner's permission, because they're very expensive. For now, I think it's better for me to treat the symptoms until she comes back."

"What can we do?" asked Neil.

"Well, you could help by keeping a close eye on him and seeing if you can identify anything that might be setting it off," Mike replied. "Examine his pen, his bedding, and change his diet, too. It could be that they've changed the formula in the dog food. You never know."

As Mike was putting away his stethoscope in his

bag, he paused for a moment before lifting out a dog collar and leash. He stared at them thoughtfully.

"Whose are those?" asked Emily.

"They're Jasper's," said Mike.

Neil lay Pepé back in his basket and slowly took both items from the vet.

"Sergeant Moorhead left them in the clinic," said Mike. "I was going to drop them off at the police station this morning, but I didn't have time."

Neil fought back a spasm of grief. "I'll take them to him," he offered. Neil had wanted to talk to the sergeant about what sort of a dog he was looking for as Jasper's replacement. Maybe he, or the King Street Kennels web site, could help the police find him a new dog. "Dad and I were already going into town later. Don't worry, I'll make sure he gets them."

Mike nodded solemnly. "Thanks, Neil."

As Neil and Emily entered the small reception area of the modern redbrick police station in Compton, Neil immediately spotted a familiar head of reddish hair. It was Mr. Harding.

With a sense of shock, Neil realized that it had been nearly a year since he had last seen the ex-policeman. He remembered the frightening time when he was all alone with a tied-up Harding in a remote cottage, waiting for the police to arrive. Harding's dog, Jessie, had chosen that moment to go into labor. It had been touch and go for Jessie for a while, until Mike had operated on her and delivered the three pups.

"Look, there's Mr. Harding," whispered Emily.

"I don't want him to see me," Neil hissed and looked away. "He might be mad at me for getting him sent to prison!"

But it was too late.

Harding had seen them. He said something to the duty officer who was manning the reception desk, then came over, looking rather sheepish.

Bob Parker arrived behind Neil and locked eyes with Mr. Harding.

"Er, hello, Mr. Parker," said Harding. "Hello, Neil. I gather you and your dad were a great help to Sergeant Moorhead the other night. . . ."

"I hear you were, too," Bob replied with a very frosty expression on his face.

Neil glanced up at his dad, then at Mr. Harding. Neil could tell he wasn't at all pleased to be confronted by the ex-policeman. Neil had been in a great deal of danger back then, and his parents blamed Mr. Harding.

"I'm just waiting for the sergeant to arrive," Harding said. "I've got some fresh information for him."

"Really?" said Bob.

"Yes, but I'd like a word with you first."

Neil froze. Was Mr. Harding about to be angry

with him for handing him over to the police like he did? He decided to get in first. "Look, if it's about what happened, I had to do it —"

Harding shook his head. "Neil, don't worry. There are no hard feelings. I know you had to. I did wrong and was punished. Let's forget what's past, OK?" Neil thought Mr. Harding looked sincere — but he'd been misled by that expression before. "No, it's something different I wanted to talk to you about," Harding continued. "It's about Jessie. I've never really thanked you for what you did for her . . ."

Mr. Harding looked really uncomfortable, and Neil almost felt sorry for him. Despite everything that had happened, Neil couldn't help liking Mr. Harding — even though he was a criminal. Anybody who had witnessed his love and concern for Jessie, and the Airedale cross's obvious devotion to him, would have known Harding to be a true dog lover. And Neil had all the time in the world for dog lovers.

"What happened to her pups, Mr. Harding?" Neil asked.

"They were real beauties." Mr. Harding's eyes shone with pride. "They all found good homes. But it's thanks to you that they were born at all."

"I'd love to see Jessie again," said Neil. The words were out of his mouth before he could stop himself.

Emily gulped and Bob suddenly glared at him.

Neil couldn't help it, though. He'd grown so attached to Jessie during her stay at King Street Kennels and he *did* long to see her again. After Harding's arrest, his sister had taken Jessie in, but Neil was glad that she and her beloved master were now reunited.

"I'm sure Jessie would like to see you again, too," said Harding. "Why don't you and your father drop by someday soon? Even this afternoon, if you can make it. I know Barbara would be pleased to meet you."

"Who's Barbara?" Neil asked. "Have you got another dog?"

Harding laughed. "No, she's my wife. We got married just a month ago, but we've known each other for years. We're living here in Compton now. In Forthlyn Grove, on the edge of town. Do you know it?"

Neil nodded. "I'd love to come," he said, trying to avoid his father's eyes. He knew his dad wouldn't be at all happy to go.

Just then, Sergeant Moorhead came in. Bob was the first to greet him and ask how he was.

"Very sad," he replied. "I've had dogs before, but never one like Jasper. The dog that replaces him will have to be really special."

Neil stepped forward. "Sergeant, Mike asked me to bring these in for you. You left them at the clinic," Neil said. He handed over the collar and leash and saw the sorrow in the sergeant's eyes as he thanked him.

"I'll let you know if I hear of a suitable dog. How old does he have to be?" Bob asked the sergeant.

"Under a year. The sooner his training can start, the better." Then Sergeant Moorhead spotted Harding, who was waiting by the desk. "I'd better go and see what news he's brought me," he said. "And Neil . . . thanks for these." He lifted up Jasper's collar and leash. "I'll keep them as a souvenir of the best dog I've ever known."

CHAPTER FOUR

Over lunch that day, Neil tried hard to persuade his father to let him visit Jessie and Mr. Harding. "But Dad, he's OK now — he's helping the police, he's on their side," he argued.

Bob seemed reluctant to trust him. "I'm not so sure," he insisted. "Don't you think it could be more than coincidence that he just happened to be passing by on Thursday night while the robbery was going on? He could have been involved in the robbery. That would mean that he might be partly to blame for Jasper's death!"

"No way!" exclaimed Neil. "He loves dogs. Look how good he is to Jessie! He'd never do anything to hurt one. I don't think he had anything to do with it."

Bob gave a grunt of disagreement.

"All I want is to go and see Jessie, just once," he said.

"Me, too," Emily said eagerly.

"What do you think, Mom?" asked Neil.

"Well, I suppose he'd hardly be likely to arrive on a motorcycle if he was the getaway man at the scene of a crime!" said Carole.

"Exactly," said Neil. "He's got a wife now, too. He's got a new life. I'm sure he's made a fresh start, Dad."

"He did put you in a great deal of danger, Neil," said Bob. "But, I suppose a wife might be a good influence on him. . . ."

"Like I am on you, you mean?" Carole teased Bob.

"What do you think, Sam?" Neil turned to the Border collie, who was noisily scratching himself.

Sam looked at Neil and barked. Neil laughed. "Remember Jessie?" he said. Sam's ears pricked up. "Would you like to see Jessie again, Sam? One bark for no, two for yes."

It was a long time since Neil had used the signs he had taught Sam. He didn't know if he would remember them. He had taught him to "count" by moving his paw in a certain way — once for one bark, twice for two, and so on. Sam's fantastic memory brought the correct response right away: "Woof, woof!"

Carole laughed. "That's not fair," she said. "How can anyone resist Sam?" Then her face grew more serious. "I've never forgotten Jessie. She was probably the best-trained dog that ever stayed here. And I don't say that lightly. I wonder if she'll ever have any more pups? She went through such a bad time giving birth, poor girl."

Neil smiled to himself. He had a feeling he was winning the battle. "Mom," he persisted, "I promise you I'll find out every detail about Jessie and let you know as soon as I come back."

Carole exchanged a stern look with Bob, but then her face softened a little and she let out a little sigh. "I suppose if your father supervised a short visit, then there would be no harm in that."

Neil and Emily smiled at each other. Success!

*   *   *

That afternoon, Neil and Emily, escorted by their dad, went to Mr. Harding's new house at Forthlyn Grove.

Neil rang the bell and called Jessie's name through the mail slot and was rewarded with an outburst of excited barking. A pretty woman with blond hair answered the door and introduced herself as Barbara Harding.

"I'm so pleased to meet you all. James has told me all about how you helped Jessie," she said. "He really is grateful to you for saving Jessie's life. Aren't you, darling?"

Mr. Harding came down the hallway behind her and stood behind his wife. "Yes, I certainly am," he said. "Now, come on. Listen to that welcome you're getting!"

Neil could hear frantic barks and thuds as Jessie tried to open the door of the living room. As soon as Harding turned the handle, she pushed her way out and ran straight to Neil, who held out his hand for her to lick.

The golden-brown Airedale cross looked the picture of health, so unlike the last time he had seen her, shortly after her pups had been delivered in Mike Turner's clinic. Then, she had looked thin and stressed. Now, she looked like a new dog. *I bet it's because Mr. Harding's back,* thought Neil, as he tangled his fingers in her curly coat. "Good girl, Jessie," he said. "Now, sit!"

Jessie obeyed immediately. Neil took a dog treat

out of his pocket and held it in the air. Jessie remained in a sitting position, though her wet black nose sniffed the air excitedly.

Emily laughed. "Poor Jessie. Look at her tail quivering."

"I bet Jake wouldn't last that long," Bob joked. "He'd have his nose in your pocket by now."

"Good girl," Neil repeated, walking backward down the hallway till he arrived at the open kitchen door. Jessie stayed absolutely still, though she glanced at Harding once or twice. "Come, Jessie, come," Neil called. In three bounds, Jessie was there, happily taking the treat from Neil's hand.

"Who got her pups, Mr. Harding?" asked Neil.

"An old colleague from my dog training days, Constable Lloyd, took the male. He called him Freddie. He's settled in really well. As for the two females, you know Marcus Welham?"

Everyone did. He was a soccer player who played for a major team and had a big house near Padsham. "Marcus has Amber and his cousin bought Dawn. They've all settled in really well."

"You've done what you came here for, you two. You've seen Jessie and found out about the pups. I think it's time we were going," Bob said. He looked uneasy, standing in the Hardings' front hall.

"You can't go yet. There's someone else I want to introduce you to," Harding said eagerly. "Come this way . . ."

Neil and Emily went with Harding, and Bob had no choice but to follow.

Mr. Harding led them all out of the kitchen into an extension that had been turned into a very professional-looking dog kennel with two pens. One was empty, but in the other was a young, very furry German shepherd, who cocked his head to one side and wagged his tail in a friendly greeting.

"Meet Sherlock. I *hope* he's going to be Compton's next police dog," announced Harding.

"Cool!" said Neil, crouching down in front of the pen. "What a great dog. How old is he?"

"Eleven months," Harding replied. "He belonged to a dog breeder I used to know when I worked for the London Met. He's just had to retire because of illness."

"What age are police dogs when they start training?" Emily wanted to know.

"If they're taken on as puppies, they go and live with their handlers at about three months. They're assessed thoroughly at around ten months, and when they're about a year old, they start their real training.

"Sherlock's a natural. He's taken to everything, especially tracking. Police dogs have to be able to search all kinds of different places — buildings, open countryside, woods, to recover missing kids, property — you name it. Sherlock's so eager to work, it's almost unbelievable," Harding said fondly.

"Why don't you let him live in the house with

you?" asked Bob. Neil gave his dad a sharp look. Despite his reservations, his dad was obviously interested in finding out more about Sherlock, too.

"He mustn't get spoiled. He is, first and foremost, a working dog. He comes in for a while every day. The rest of the time is spent working him and playing with him. Both are equally important," Harding explained.

"Can I have a look at him?" asked Neil.

"Sure." Mr. Harding opened the door of the pen. "Stay," he ordered. Sherlock's ears flicked. There was no mistaking the intelligence and understanding in his amber eyes. But he stayed, even though he must have been dying to run out into the yard.

"Here," Harding said.

Sherlock bounded out of the kennel and sat by Harding's feet. Jessie came up and sniffed him and the two dogs rubbed noses. Neil offered his fingers to be sniffed, then stroked Sherlock's head. He half expected Sherlock to jump up, but he remained where he was, although he pricked his ears and looked up at Neil.

"He's very obedient," said Emily. "When's he going to go and live with Sergeant Moorhead?"

"Er, the sergeant doesn't know about him yet. It didn't seem right, so soon after Jasper's death," Harding replied.

"You're not a police dog trainer anymore. Will they still take a dog from you?" asked Bob.

"They know I *was* a good trainer. And the police do try out dogs offered to them by members of the public or recognized dog dealers. They're always short of talented dogs, and if a dog shows he's intelligent enough and has the right personality, they may take him on for training. They're very choosy because it costs more than six thousand pounds to train a police dog and they don't want to waste their money," explained Mr. Harding.

"Do they only take males, or do they train females as well?" Emily wanted to know.

"Either. Some forces prefer males, but females can make excellent police dogs, too."

Emily got down and made a fuss of Sherlock, burying her face in his thick fur. He made her giggle when he licked her ear.

"It'll be tough when he goes," remarked Bob, giving Sherlock's head a stroke.

"Yes, it will. But I'd like to see him really working," Harding said.

"I'd love to see what he can do," said Neil. "Why don't you bring him over to our place sometime? We've still got Sam's old agility course."

"Maybe I'll do that," said Mr. Harding. "I'm sure Sherlock would love to show off his skills." He rubbed the thick ruff around the German shepherd's neck and was rewarded with a wet wrist. "You should see him tracking. He's great," said Harding. "In fact, I don't think I've ever worked with such a brilliant dog. Would you like to see him jump?"

There was a large, solid-looking object toward the end of the tidy, well-kept yard. "You don't mean *that*, do you?" asked Emily. "It's enormous!"

"Six feet," Harding said. "Police dogs have to be able to clear a nine-foot-long jump and a three-foot hurdle as well. Stay, Jessie!"

He gave Sherlock the order to climb the wall. Sherlock hurled himself at it and scaled it like a mountaineer, using his claws to help him. At the top, he turned his head and panted happily at his audience before leaping down on the other side.

"Good boy!" Harding exclaimed, ruffling his fur and giving him a pat.

"Wow!" said Neil. "We're impressed!"

"That *was* excellent," said Bob. "You don't want to wait too long before you tell Sergeant Moorhead about him. The force will be insisting he get another dog very soon," he warned. "I'll put in a good word, if you like . . . tell him I've seen Sherlock and that he's worth a look."

"I'm sure the sergeant will fall in love with Sherlock as soon as he sees him," said Emily.

"Falling in love with him's not the most important thing," Bob pointed out. "It's how good he is at police work that really counts. Dog and handler do have to take to each other though, so it's a combination of the two. Isn't that right, Mr. Harding?"

"Yes, that's right. If a dog and a handler didn't take to each other, the handler would be given another dog. The bond between them is extremely important. The dog has to *want* to do anything his handler might ask of him, which may include dangerous situations involving weapons."

Neil couldn't bear to think of criminals using guns or knives on dogs.

"Thanks for letting us meet Sherlock and visit with Jessie, Mr. Harding, but we really have to be getting back now," said Bob. He tugged on Neil's arm.

Neil and Emily reluctantly tore themselves away.

"Maybe I can come again to see Sherlock?" said Neil as he went back into the house.

"Maybe," replied Harding. "If it's OK with your parents."

"Maybe . . ." mumbled Bob as they said their good-byes.

CHAPTER FIVE

eil and Emily arrived back at King Street Kennels to discover their mom in an agitated state. She looked quite pale and anxious.

"We've got rats in the food storeroom," she announced.

"Yuck!" said Emily.

"And you know how much I hate them. They terrify me," Carole said with a shudder.

"What happened?" asked Bob.

"It was Kate who discovered it. Teeth marks in the bottom of sacks of dog biscuits. And they've made a real meal of the hamster food." The Parkers bought animal feed in bulk from their suppliers. "Come and see for yourselves," Carole said.

Sure enough, there was a neat hole in the bottom

of the sack of Fudge's food and a little heap of nuts and seeds on the concrete floor.

"Oh, no!" Bob exploded. "Rats are all we need. If a customer were to see one, we could lose our good name."

"We can't put poison down, though, because of the dogs," Carole pointed out.

"How about getting a dog to do some ratting for us? Maybe we could borrow Tuff," suggested Neil. Tuff was a Jack Russell terrier that belonged to a local farmer, Harry Grey. Jack Russells had a reputation for being good ratters and Tuff was one of the best.

"It's an idea," said Bob. "But I'm not at all sure Harry will be able to spare him. He's got too many rats and mice of his own, and Tuff would have to live here for a while."

"Too bad," said Neil. "I'm sure he would have enjoyed it."

"What are we going to do, then?" asked Carole.

"How about getting a cat?" Emily piped up.

"We couldn't possibly have a cat," snapped Carole. "It would drive the dogs crazy."

"Where's Kate?" Bob asked Carole. "We should ask her if she's actually seen one of these rats. We should be sure it is what we think it is."

"Oh, I gave her the rest of the day off," Carole replied. "She seems pretty depressed."

"*She's* depressed? What about *us*?" demanded Bob. "We're going to lose her and she'll be hard to replace. I still think we could help her change her mind."

Neil exchanged glances with Emily. They'd tried to corner her several times to help persuade her themselves, but hadn't had the chance. Someone else had distracted them, or the phone had rung, or she was just too busy to talk.

Just before dinner, Neil and Emily got ready to go out over the hills behind the kennels to take Jake for a long walk. Emily suggested they take Pepé, too, if he hadn't already been walked, so they went to the kennel block to find out.

They found Bev tidying up before she left for the day.

"Hi, Bev," said Neil. "Has Pepé been for his walk yet?"

Bev's blue eyes twinkled. "Not yet. I was sort of saving him for you," she said.

"That's great! I'll get his leash. D'you want us to take any of the others while we're at it?"

"I think Pepé will be quite enough. That little dog's like a jumping bean. He doesn't need vitamins — I think he's got springs in his paws," she grumbled.

Twilight was falling as Neil and Emily brought the dogs back to King Street. Pepé and Jake had both disgraced themselves in various ways, Jake by rolling in mud and Pepé by trying to wriggle down a rabbit hole.

"You're a Chihuahua, not a dachshund," Neil had to remind him as he grabbed him by the wiggling hindquarters and dragged him out.

Neil put Pepé back in his pen in Kennel Block Two. He was just walking back across the courtyard to join Emily in the kitchen, when Jake suddenly gave a loud, excited bark and went dashing off in pursuit of something.

"Jake! Come here!" he called, but Jake took no notice.

The young collie skidded to a halt by the garden gate. Whatever it was had obviously gotten away under the gate — and had headed in the direction of their house!

Neil opened the gate and Jake ran inside. He stopped by Sam's favorite bush, then sniffed and whined. Neil couldn't see a thing in the fading light, so he shrugged his shoulders and gave up, ushering Jake inside into the warmth of the kitchen.

The following morning, Neil got up and found his father in a seething rage.

"Look at that!" he shouted, pointing out of the window into the backyard.

Neil looked. "What is it? I can't see anything."

"On the lawn!" thundered Bob.

Neil looked at the grass. There, leading from the very bush Jake had stopped at the previous night, was a neat row of molehills. He burst out laughing. He couldn't help it. His father looked at him furiously. "It's not funny," he complained.

"Yes it is," Neil replied and told his dad what had happened the previous night. "I took it for granted that Jake had seen a rat, but it was probably just a mole," he said.

"Moles eat insects. They don't eat grain or dog food," said Carole.

"I think we should set a trap in the feed storeroom," suggested Neil.

"I don't know about that, but there's a certain young pup that needs to be led over to Red's Barn soon. My obedience class starts in half an hour. Don't be late," Bob reminded him.

Neil and Emily usually helped clean out the kennels on Sunday morning. They went in search of Kate and saw her heading for the rescue center. "Quick, she's alone!" said Neil. It was the ideal opportunity to launch their campaign to stop Kate from leaving.

They cornered Kate in one of the vacated pens, where she was up to her elbows in soapsuds and water.

"Hi, Kate," Neil greeted her. "We've come to help."

"That's good. I could certainly use some." Kate

looked up and smiled, tossing her blond ponytail
back over her shoulder.

Neil had planned to work up to the subject of her
leaving gradually, but Emily preempted him.

"We can't believe you want to leave King Street!"
she cried, sounding close to tears.

Kate went red. "Hang on, I don't know if I am leaving yet. I don't know if the SPCA will hire me," she
said.

"Aren't you happy with us?" Emily continued in a
choked voice.

"Of course I am," Kate replied. "But nobody can do the same thing forever. We all need a change sometimes. Anyway, the SPCA building is near where Glen lives." Glen was Kate's boyfriend.

"Oh, so Glen's the real reason," Neil said. "What a relief. We thought you were leaving because of Bev."

They waited for Kate's reply. She avoided their eyes and carried on playing with her hair. Then, finally, she said, "Bev *has* got something to do with it. I mean, I really like her and she's great with the dogs. Too good, that's the trouble. She's much better than me."

"Don't be silly! You're both good at different things. That's why you're such a good team. We can't do without either of you. We really want you to stay, Kate. We'd miss you terribly if you left. So would the dogs."

Neil realized his words were falling on deaf ears as Kate lowered her eyes and busied herself with her cleaning. She was obviously dead set on getting the SPCA job, and there was nothing anyone could do about it.

There were five dogs in Bob's obedience class that Sunday morning. Jake was one of them, and Neil was pleased when the young Border collie appeared to respond to Bob's command to be quiet and stop barking.

The class was just ending when Carole walked up

to the barn with Sergeant Moorhead. It was just a social call, the sergeant said. They were still searching for the thief who'd killed Jasper, and they hadn't found the car yet.

"We're grateful to Mr. Harding for getting the car's license plate number for us. Here it is. If you happen to spot it on your travels, let me know right away," said the sergeant, writing the license number down for them. Bob and Neil promised they would.

This seemed like a perfect opportunity to tell the sergeant about Sherlock. Neil mouthed his name and his father gave him the nod.

"Has Mr. Harding mentioned a dog called Sherlock to you?" asked Neil.

Sergeant Moorhead shook his head.

"He's a German shepherd and he's brilliant. Mr. Harding's training him. I really think you should see him," Neil said eagerly.

"I would have liked to, but it's too late, I'm afraid."

Neil's heart sank.

The sergeant went on. "I know it's only three days since Jasper was killed, but the force has already arranged to have a dog sent to me who's currently in the middle of his training. I'm obligated to give him the first chance, I'm afraid. If he and I like each other, then that's it. His name's Oliver," the sergeant said. "He's arriving next weekend."

Neil brightened up again. If Oliver wasn't arriving for another week, then they had seven days to get

Sherlock and the sergeant together. There had to be some way of doing it. Once he saw Sherlock, he was bound to be hooked and Oliver would have to find another handler to work with.

"Come on, Em. Get your thinking cap on," Neil urged his sister. "There must be something we can come up with."

They were both in the kitchen sneaking hot chocolate and cookies before their lunch.

"We could invite Mr. Harding to come to the kennel with Sherlock," suggested Emily, "when we know Sergeant Moorhead's going to be here . . ."

Neil dismissed Emily's idea. "We *never* know when he's going to be here, silly! He just pops in when he's off duty. It's hopeless making any arrangements with him because he's likely to get called out on a case at any moment."

Emily snorted with annoyance. Then she said, "OK, I've got it. Mrs. Harding can invite Sergeant Moorhead over for tea and chocolate cake, then Mr. Harding could show him Sherlock."

Neil sighed. "Why would he want to go there for tea? They're not exactly best buddies, are they? Anyway, he needs to be able to see Sherlock in action."

They sat in grumpy silence, broken only by Sam loudly lapping water out of his bowl. Jake whined to be let in, so Emily opened the door and he scampered into the kitchen, wagging his tail excitedly.

Neil scolded him when he jumped up and put his front paws on the table leg. "Down, Jake," he ordered. Neil laughed and scratched him between the ears, then ruffled the long, silky fur on his chest. "Will you never learn?" he said with exasperation.

Neil and Emily decided to take Jake and Sam for a walk. Their mother was in the field, exercising some of the rescue dogs.

"Your father can't stop talking about Sherlock," she said. "I would love to see him."

"But you can, Mom," Neil told her. "All you have to do is ask Mr. Harding. He'd love to show him off to you."

"I can't go over *there*," his mother replied.

"Why not?" Neil said. "You'd really enjoy talking to him. He knows an awful lot about dogs."

"The trouble is, I still have this thing about him," Carole confessed. "I can't help it. He put you in so much danger, Neil, and I'm not sure I want to become friendly with him. On the other hand, I'd like to see Jessie again. I'm hoping it won't be long before her pups become regular boarders of ours."

"Marcus Welham is away a lot. If his wife goes with him, we might get Amber to look after," Emily said hopefully.

"Why don't we invite Mr. Harding to come here? He never looked around much before. He could see the kennels and bring Sherlock and Jessie with him, and you could watch Sherlock go around Sam's old agility course, if we can find all the pieces. Then you wouldn't have to make it a special occasion."

Carole looked thoughtful. "I suppose that would be OK. We'd be keeping things on a professional footing then, rather than making it personal."

"Can he come this afternoon? I can't wait to see Sherlock again," Emily said.

"No. I've got far too much to do. Anyway, you only saw him yesterday," her mother replied. "Next weekend, perhaps . . ."

Both Neil and Emily would have been happy to see Sherlock and Jessie every day of the week, but they knew next weekend would have to do. It was very frustrating to have to wait so long.

CHAPTER SIX

On Monday, Carole Parker was just starting the car to take Neil and his sisters to school when the phone rang.

Neil picked it up. It was Miss Thorn, the school secretary, and she sounded extremely harassed. She explained that there were some burst pipes in the main school building and the heat wouldn't work. School had to be canceled for the day while the plumbers were called in.

Neil, Emily, and Sarah couldn't believe their luck. Another day of freedom!

"Perhaps we could ask Mr. Harding to come today," Neil suggested when they regrouped in the kitchen.

"Yes, please," echoed Emily and Sarah.

Their father was soon brought into the discussion.

"I know your mother's dying to see if Sherlock's as good as we think he is . . . so, OK!"

Neil was delighted to discover that Mr. Harding was free to come and visit. He seemed excited by the opportunity to show off Sherlock to Bob and Carole, who were such influential people in the local dog business. A couple of hours later, Neil rushed out of the house to greet him when he heard the car pull up outside the house.

Mr. Harding walked with Jessie and Sherlock to the back of the house. Jessie seemed to recognize King Street Kennels immediately and soon ran around sniffing familiar smells and wagging her tail. She and Sam rubbed noses, but Jake surprised everyone by gluing himself to Jessie. He insisted on following her everywhere, giving little whines of pleasure when she licked him.

"He thinks he's one of her puppies," Mr. Harding said.

Neil was relieved to see that Jake's adoration of Jessie really helped break the ice as far as his mother was concerned. She soon warmed to Jessie, and Neil could tell she found it difficult not to take an interest in the dog's well-being. "Are you going to let Jessie have another litter?" Carole asked.

"No. She went through enough the last time. She's been spayed now," Mr. Harding replied.

Sherlock looked magnificent. Neil crouched down and rubbed him under the chin while the German shepherd fixed his keen amber eyes on him. Carole adored him from the get-go. She crouched down and examined him, looking at his eyes and the way he held his tail. She took a professional glance inside his mouth. "I can see that you clean his teeth," she said approvingly to Mr. Harding. "You'd be surprised how many dog owners don't."

Bev and Kate came out to see who the visitors were and laughed at the antics of Jessie and Jake. Sam had gone back to the house and was lying in a rare patch of sunshine by the back door.

While Bev, Kate, and Carole showed Mr. Harding around, Neil asked his father to help him dig out all the old obstacles Sam used to practice agility training on. It took quite a while to set up the plank and the jumps, then Neil went to get everyone.

Mr. Harding led Sherlock into the field. The dog sat at his owner's feet, his eyes sparkling with excitement. His ears were pricked as he waited to be given the command to start.

As soon as his master spoke, Sherlock sped off like a rocket, with Mr. Harding running alongside him, giving him instructions and encouragement.

"Wow, look at him jump!" Emily shouted excitedly as Sherlock flew over the long jump.

The German shepherd was just approaching the hastily constructed wall, which Bob had helped to shore up, when all at once a shadow appeared at his side — a sinuous, speeding, black-and-white one. As

Sherlock made a leap for the top of the wall, another dog made it to the top before him and Neil gave a horrified cry. "Sam, no!"

With a hollow, sick feeling he watched the Border collie leap lightly down and run along the plank, showing the German shepherd the way. Then he ran over to Neil and sat at his feet, his pink tongue lolling and his ears pricked as if he were saying, "Aren't I clever?"

Emily was too horrified to speak.

"Neil!" thundered his father. "Didn't you make sure Sam couldn't get out of the kitchen?"

"But, Dad . . ." began Neil, faltering as he gently stroked the panting collie beside him.

"No buts. It was your responsibility to make sure Sam was shut safely indoors. You know how he loves obstacle courses. This is exactly what we don't want him to do."

Before Sam's heart condition had been diagnosed, Neil used to enter the dog in every agility contest going. Sam adored them. But getting too excited was a serious risk to his health.

Neil had to forget about watching Sherlock complete the course as he walked Sam back to the house. His father's ominous parting words rang in his ears. "Calm Sam down before he collapses again." Neil couldn't help thinking that if anything happened to Sam now, it would be all his fault.

Neil sat with Sam for the rest of the afternoon, but he didn't appear to have suffered any ill effects from his sudden burst of strenuous activity — the very thing Mike Turner had insisted Sam must avoid.

Bev found Neil in the living room and checked that Sam was OK. "You really missed something after you went in," she said. "Your mother wanted to see Sherlock do some tracking, so they let him sniff one of Sarah's gloves. Then Mr. Harding led Sherlock away so that he couldn't see Sarah trailing her glove across the field and hiding it. He followed the scent, nose to the ground, and went straight for it. It was amazing."

Neil sighed. "I wish I'd been there," he said.

Bev gave Sam a long stroke from his head down to the tip of his tail. "Poor old thing," she said.

Then Sarah came rushing in and threw her arms around Bev, nearly sending her flying. Sarah adored the new kennel assistant.

"Come on, little one. Let's take Jake for a walk, shall we?" she suggested, sensing that Neil would rather be left alone with Sam. Bev was uncannily good at figuring out the moods of both humans and dogs. Emily thought she was a bit psychic.

"I missed saying good-bye to Sherlock. And Jessie," Neil said when his mother came back to the house.

"I'm sure you'll be seeing them again. It's this old guy you need to concentrate on for the time being," she said. She knelt down beside Sam and checked his heart rate against her wristwatch.

"He's been fine this afternoon," said Neil.

Carole nodded. "Good," she said.

"So were you impressed with Sherlock, then?" asked Neil.

Carole smiled. "Very. He'll be as good a dog as Jessie soon. Mr. Harding's a very good trainer, I have to admit it."

"I know," said Neil.

"He has good instincts about dogs, too. You know the problem we're having with Mickey howling at night? Well, he asked me if we knew who Mickey's previous owner had been. When I said he used to belong to a factory night-shift worker, Mr. Harding guessed what the problem might be."

"And what's that?" Neil wasn't sure what she was getting at.

"Well, he figured that Mickey was used to being alone at night but probably had a radio or television left on as company for him."

"That's really smart!" exclaimed Neil.

"Yes, it is," admitted Carole.

"So I suppose you want me to loan you my portable radio," sighed Neil. "It'll cost you, though."

"OK, what's the cost?" Carole inquired with a grin.

"A new set of batteries," Neil replied.

"It's a deal!"

Mr. Harding's suggestion for silencing Mickey worked like a charm, and the Parkers — and the dogs, too — had a peaceful night's sleep for the first time in more than a week. Bob had attached Neil's small portable radio to the roof of Mickey's pen where he couldn't reach it — just in case he tried to change the channel with his teeth.

The heat had been fixed at Meadowbank School so it was back to school on Tuesday — unless any more pipes burst, which is what everyone was hoping for. At recess that day, Neil told his friends Chris and Hasheem all about Sherlock.

"He sounds terrific," Hasheem said. "I wish I could see him in action."

"Yes. I'd love to see what police dogs can do," Chris said longingly.

Neil stared at his friend. "I think you've just given me a really good idea . . ." he said.

After school, Neil ran his idea past Emily. She thought it was great. "So you'd get someone from the police to give a talk about what police dogs do," she confirmed.

Neil nodded energetically. "Yup."

"Then have a demonstration here at the kennel, and get Mr. Harding to bring Sherlock . . ."

"Correct. That way Sergeant Moorhead can see how good he is," Neil said. "I'm sure Compton's very own police dog handler will want to give a talk."

"Even if he hasn't got a dog at the moment?" said Emily pointedly.

Neil frowned. "Depends on how soon we can do it. Obviously, I'd like to do it before Oliver arrives," he said.

"Who's going to come to the demonstration? You can't invite all of Compton — we haven't got room!"

"I thought we could restrict it to two or three classes from school," Neil suggested. His own, Chris's, and Emily's for instance . . .

"Do you think Mom and Dad will agree?" asked Emily.

"I'm sure they will," Neil said. "They're as interested in Sergeant Moorhead having Sherlock as we are. They've really come around to the idea that Mr. Harding is a reformed character."

Bob Parker was out, so Neil went to find his mother. He found her in the office with Bev and Kate. All three looked downcast.

"What's wrong?" Neil asked in concern.

"It's this, Neil," Kate said, waving a letter in the air. "The SPCA wants me to go for an interview on Friday."

"Oh, no!" said Neil. He knew it was the wrong thing to say as soon as he saw Kate's stricken face. He could tell she felt torn in two over it. "Well, good luck, then," he said reluctantly and backed out of the room.

He was wondering what to do next when he heard the sound of a dog coughing. When he went to investigate Kennel Block Two, he found Pepé having another one of his attacks. He ran back to the office to alert the others.

Mike Turner's office number was busy and his cell phone was only taking messages.

"We'd better take Pepé right over there," Carole instructed.

Bob had taken the car, so Carole ran for the Range Rover. Neil jumped in beside her and Bev handed him a carrier containing Pepé.

Janice, Mike's veterinary nurse, greeted them at the clinic with a sympathetic glance toward Pepé.

"Poor little guy," she murmured when she saw the quivering Chihuahua. "He's so cute. Mike's doing an emergency operation at the moment, so I'll just find Pepé's notes. I can give him an injection, if that's what worked last time."

It worked extremely quickly and, by the time Mike appeared from the operating room, Pepé was almost back to normal.

"Did you see anything this time?" he said to Carole.

She shook her head. "We were all in the office when it happened, I'm afraid. We can't watch him all the time, but we did change his basket and checked his food like you said."

"OK. When's his owner coming for him?" asked Mike. "I really need to do these tests."

"On Sunday," Neil told him.

"Then I think you'll just have to set up a video camera and film what's going on," said Mike. "Something is definitely bothering him."

Neil had just started to say, "Hey, Mom, that's not a bad idea," when he realized the vet was only joking.

It had been another close call, and they were nowhere nearer to finding out the solution. It was another thing to add to Neil's list of things that were bothering him. He wanted to find a way to persuade Kate to stay at King Street Kennels *and* he still had to discuss the subject of the police dog demonstration with his parents.

CHAPTER SEVEN

Mr. Hamley, Meadowbank School's principal, had a flighty Dalmatian named Dotty. He loved dogs, but in small doses, and Dotty's recent litter had proved a bit too much for Mr. Hamley and his wife, on top of their newborn son. So Neil was careful how he phrased his plan for the police dog demonstration when he suggested it to him on Wednesday.

As it happened, he had no need to worry. Mr. Hamley thought the idea was great — very educational. He was sure it would raise him a notch or two in the school board's estimation, and Neil was only too willing to give him credit for the idea. After all, he had a different motive, and there might be a better chance of the demonstration happening if Mr. Hamley phoned the police and was the one to make the suggestion to them.

He and Emily had been right in guessing that their parents would have no objections. Their father even offered to give the exercise field its first haircut of the year with his big rider mower.

"Shouldn't you have asked Mr. Harding what he thought about showing Sherlock off before making all these plans?" Bob Parker asked Neil.

"Yes, of course I should have. I didn't think," Neil said sheepishly.

"I can't imagine that he'll raise any objection," Bob continued. "Not if it might result in finding Sherlock a home with Sergeant Moorhead. As a matter of fact, I'm dropping by to see him tonight. I'm thinking of starting an advanced obedience class, and there are one or two questions on dog training I need to ask him. Would you like to come?"

"Awesome!" Neil told his father. It was a very good sign that Bob was actually going to see Mr. Harding of his own accord. It showed that he was beginning to like him more — or at least admire his skill with dogs.

At Forthlyn Grove later that evening, Bob and Neil were greeted by two dogs trying to open the door between them. Jessie and Sherlock. A fashionably dressed Barbara stood behind them. "Good thing I'm a dog lover," she commented, "otherwise I'd get sick of removing dog hairs from my business suits."

"What do you do, exactly?" Bob asked while Neil was patting Sherlock and Jessie.

"Didn't James tell you? I own the bridal shop in Padsham. It's the only one for miles, so I don't do badly! I'm planning to invest some money to help set up James's new dog-breeding business, if we can find the right place for it."

"Maybe I can help you find somewhere, if you tell me exactly what you need," Bob offered. "That's where our web site comes in handy."

This is getting better and better, thought Neil. It would be great to see Mr. Harding succeed at what he was best at — training dogs. He certainly hadn't succeeded at being an antiques thief! Neil fed Jessie a dog treat. She was one of his favorite dogs ever, but Sherlock was quickly endearing himself to Neil, too, especially when he put a paw gently on his knee and lowered his head for Neil to scratch behind his ears. His amber eyes were the brightest that Neil had ever seen — full of warmth, intelligence, and playfulness. He really was a very special dog.

When Neil brought up the idea of a police dog demonstration, Mr. Harding was very enthusiastic. "Let me know the date as soon as you can, so I can have Sherlock looking his very best," he said. He asked Neil how Sam was, and seemed genuinely relieved to find out that he hadn't suffered any ill effects from his sudden burst of activity.

"Mrs. Harding said you wanted to start breeding dogs," Neil said. He was dying to hear more.

"Yes, that's right. I'd like to breed working dogs, such as German shepherds and spaniels, and train them."

"Spaniels?" questioned Neil. "Why spaniels?"

"They're used by the customs departments at airports and seaports because they're good at sniffing out bags and containers," Harding explained.

"I suppose the police won't have you back as a trainer now," Bob Parker said.

Harding shook his head. "Not now that I've got a criminal record. I still don't see why I can't work as a private trainer, though, and I can do that at a very high professional standard."

Much to Neil's surprise, when they got up to go, Bob said, "Well, thanks for the tea, Barbara. Goodbye, James. I'll be seeing you."

His father's use of their first names was a really good sign, Neil realized. It was too bad his mother was still so suspicious of Mr. Harding, though. The only thing that could bring her around was dogs. If Harding were to start his business, she'd be bound to show some interest in that, surely.

On Thursday morning, Mr. Hamley made a surprise announcement during assembly.

"I'm pleased to announce a special event for all Meadowbank dog lovers," he said, standing on stage at the front of the auditorium.

Neil's eyes scanned the hall for Emily, Chris, and Hasheem and they all exchanged excited glances.

"The police dog section has agreed to do some demonstrations especially for our school," continued Mr. Hamley. "Inspector Williams, who is head of the dog section in this area, will give a talk on the work of police dogs, and you'll get the chance to see a police dog being put through the agility course by his trainer. You all know Compton's very own police dog expert, Sergeant Moorhead? Well, he'll be there that day, too, to answer any questions you may have."

Mr. Hamley tapped the podium for quiet. "We've

been able to arrange the first demonstration on very short notice. It will take place tomorrow afternoon at King Street Kennels," Mr. Hamley continued. "We'll have a lottery to decide who'll be going, and you can take consent forms home this evening. Those unlucky enough not to attend this event will have the opportunity to see another similar demonstration later in the year."

Neil's brain did some swift calculations. Sergeant Moorhead had told them that he would be getting Oliver over the weekend. The demonstration was due to take place on Friday, so it looked as if his dream of getting Sherlock and Sergeant Moorhead together before Oliver came on the scene was about to come true!

That night, Neil and Emily helped their father clean up the exercise field and modernize Sam's old agility course. Sergeant Moorhead came down to inspect it and to offer them advice, and together they succeeded in constructing a very professional-looking course for the police dog demonstration.

After the sergeant had left, Neil and Emily accompanied their mother on a trip into Compton to the supermarket. As they pulled away from the parking lot, the Range Rover laden with groceries, Neil asked a question that had been eating away at him. "Mom, if the police are running the event, will they let Sherlock go over the course, too?" he asked worriedly.

"Don't worry!" she said reassuringly. "Your dad has already phoned Inspector Williams about it. He doesn't mind at all if we take a couple of our own dogs around the course."

Neil grinned with relief. "Let's take Jake around it, for a laugh," he said. "Every show needs a comedian!"

"I don't think so!" said Carole. Then she frowned. "It's a shame about Kate having her interview tomorrow afternoon. We really need every bit of help we can get."

"Couldn't she ask them to change the day?" Emily asked hopefully.

Neil felt the same way. It depressed him every time he thought about Kate and her interview. It seemed that she just didn't want to listen to any argument that might help persuade her to stay at King Street.

"I don't think she wants to change it, to be honest," said Carole. "This business has taken so much emotional energy out of all of us that I think she just wants it over with now. We all do. But she has promised to come right back as soon as it's over."

Suddenly, Emily pointed a finger toward the window. "Oh, look, Neil!"

The car was going past Compton police station and Neil turned around to see what his sister had noticed. Sergeant Moorhead was getting out of a van — with a dog. A young German shepherd. His heart sank. "Oh, no," he groaned. "That must be Oliver!"

Carole slowed the vehicle a little and everyone craned across to look at the new arrival.

"This is a disaster!" said Emily. "Oliver wasn't expected until Sunday!"

"Sergeant Moorhead didn't mention anything earlier about getting Oliver tonight!" cried Neil. "Just look at him."

They all watched as the well-built German shepherd obeyed the sergeant's commands to follow him into the station building.

Neil had to admit to himself that the dog looked healthy and well muscled. He was very athletic-looking, too, for such a young dog. This was Neil's worst nightmare. All of their efforts might now be in vain.

As soon as he got home, Neil told his father what they had seen at the police station. "We might as well cancel the demonstration now," Neil said miserably.

"Of course we can't!" exclaimed Bob. "Your schoolmates would be really disappointed, and we can't fool around with the police like that. They have no idea about your reasons for wanting this show so badly."

"But there's no point in having it now," said Neil glumly. "It's too late! The whole thing was about getting Sergeant Moorhead together with Sherlock, but he's got Oliver now."

"It's never too late," Bob insisted. "The sergeant and Oliver may not get along. That's what being a dog handler's all about — the right dog with the right man. It's like a marriage. It needs the right chemistry, and Oliver and Sergeant Moorhead may not have it."

"I hope they don't," Neil replied.

"They're bound to see Sherlock's talent, anyway," added Bob.

"I haven't got anything *against* Oliver," said Neil. "I haven't even met him yet, and he does look like a great dog. But I really, *really* want Sherlock to be Compton's police dog, and I thought I'd fixed it when I had the idea for the demonstration. I feel really frustrated now."

Bob shrugged. "Life's not always very fair," he commented.

"No, it certainly isn't," Neil agreed. "If it was, Jasper wouldn't have been killed and Sergeant Moorhead wouldn't have to find his killer." He paused and heaved a great sigh. Then he got to his feet. "I'm going to take Sam for a walk," he said. He needed to get some fresh air and work through his agitated feelings. Sam's calm presence was the perfect medicine for his troubles.

While the agility course was laid out for the demonstration the following day, Neil thought it best to take Sam everywhere on a leash. Otherwise, no one could have kept him off it!

"It's only for a couple more days, boy," said Neil, stroking Sam's gleaming black back. Sam thumped his plumy tail on the ground and looked pointedly through the gate at the objects in the field.

"No, I *can't* let you in there," Neil said softly. "You and I will have to go for a walk in the woods instead."

Apart from two or three established tracks, the woods that ran along the length of the hillside were wild and steep and, in some places, almost impassable. When he was younger, Neil and his friend Chris Turner had spent many happy hours drawing adventure maps of the woods, filling in caves and inventing treasure, bears, wolves, and even the occasional abominable snowman.

Today, Neil and Sam took one of the regular paths. He walked slowly so Sam wouldn't tire himself by climbing too fast. He had exercised Jake earlier, to allow himself this quality time with Sam.

As he walked back toward home in the fading light, he found himself thinking about Sherlock. The dog was far too talented at police work to spend his life merely as a pet. Not that Mr. Harding would let him go to somebody who would pamper and spoil him. He'd be more likely to keep him himself. But surely some police force somewhere would recognize his talent and be prepared to take him on?

Maybe Inspector Williams, the head of dog training, would talent-scout him. If he couldn't become the Compton police dog, maybe the Colshaw or Padsham forces would have him. But then Neil wouldn't see him anymore. No, Sherlock *had* to become Compton's police dog.

CHAPTER EIGHT

It seemed strange to Neil to have to spend Friday morning in school as usual, then come back to his own home accompanied by a teacher!

The weather forecast predicted a dry afternoon, so Mr. Hamley and Mrs. Sharpe, his class teacher, helped unload the school PA system from the school bus to set it up in the field. Bob had borrowed stacks of folding chairs from Gavin Thorpe at the church hall and set them up in neat lines.

Just after two o'clock, Inspector Williams, head of the area police dog section, began his talk, flanked by two experienced dog handlers and their dogs. Both were German shepherds — one was named Rusty and looked about six months older than Sherlock. She had just completed her basic training. The other was a much more mature dog, aged three, named Barney.

Neil stood on one side of the rows of chairs and watched his school friends as they eagerly absorbed the inspector's fascinating stories about life in the force with a dog. Mr. Harding was in the back of the audience with Sherlock.

At intervals, while the inspector talked, Neil looked around anxiously toward the kennels. The most important person of the afternoon was still missing. Soon, Sherlock would get his chance to show what he was capable of, but without Sergeant Moorhead there to witness it, all the German shepherd's efforts — and Neil's too — would be wasted.

Inspector Williams finished his talk and was greeted with a spontaneous round of applause.

Then Neil's father announced that a local dog would be put around the course and asked to display some tracking skills. This would be followed by a demonstration by the trained police dogs. There was an outbreak of excited chattering. This was what everyone had been looking forward to — a chance to see dogs in action.

Neil went and stood next to Mr. Harding and Sherlock, who looked eager and raring to go. "It must be difficult for a dog to follow a scent in wet grass," he remarked to Mr. Harding. "Isn't it easier if the grass is dry?"

To his surprise, Mr. Harding told him wet grass held a scent longer than dry grass. "A dog has to be able to find a person or an object as long as two hours after the scent has been laid. They have to rest their noses every twenty minutes if they're tracking over a long distance. Their sense of smell is about two hundred times better than that of a human being."

At last, everybody settled down and it was time for Sherlock to start the demonstration. Neil saw interest in the eyes of the police dog handlers as the handsome young German shepherd came up to the course. Mr. Harding gave him a pat, then led him to the first obstacle. Sherlock was like an Olympic athlete. He seemed to take wing as he did his long jump.

He cleared the three yards easily. He flew over the hurdle and managed the plank surefootedly.

When he came to the wall, the dog prepared for his leap like a horse would do in a show-jumping ring. He sized it up, then took a run up to it, followed by a mighty jump that took him in one bound almost to the very top. One heave and he was on the ridge, then down the other side, to a round of applause.

Then Mr. Harding had an opportunity to show how well Sherlock could track. Mr. Harding asked for a volunteer and Hasheem Lindon was the first to put up his hand and dash onto the field. Neil's friend let Sherlock have a good sniff of him, then was instructed to lose himself in the crowd while Sherlock's vision was covered. Hasheem sat right at the back of the spectators, but as soon as Mr. Harding issued a command, Sherlock went virtually straight to him.

Excellent! thought Neil. *That dog's just incredible! If only Sergeant Moorhead could have seen him,* Neil thought agonizingly. Then he reminded himself that there were other representatives of the dog section here, including the area headman himself. Surely they would know a first-class police dog when they saw one?

Sherlock's performance earned him a round of cheers and noisy applause. People crowded around to make a fuss over him, and the inspector came up to talk to Mr. Harding.

Suddenly, Neil noticed someone else in uniform taking a close interest in Sherlock. Someone with another German shepherd in a harness and on a leash. *Sergeant Moorhead!* Neil thought triumphantly.

How long had he been there? Neil could only assume the sergeant had arrived while he had been concentrating on watching Sherlock's accomplished performance on the field. He hoped the sergeant had witnessed the whole of Sherlock's performance.

Inspector Williams made a further announcement. "I think we were *all* impressed with Sherlock. A splendid example of dedicated training — and very much like the real thing!"

Hear, hear, thought Neil.

It was now time for the highlight of the demonstration, when one of the fully trained police dogs, Barney, gave his display. This included the "chase and attack" technique, in which a dog caught a human quarry. The police officer who was to play the role of criminal had padding around his arm, just in case, though the dogs were trained not to bite too hard.

The police officer raced down the field, then Barney was released and hurtled after him. Everyone gasped as the man pretended to fight Barney, and the German shepherd held on to his arm until his own handler could reach the spot. It was a thrilling moment.

After both dogs had excelled over the agility course with flawless performances, the police team answered lots of questions. Finally, Mr. Hamley gave a speech thanking the police and Bob Parker.

Neil listened impatiently. He was dying to tear himself away from his parents and go over to where Mr. Harding was now talking to Sergeant Moorhead! As soon as Mr. Hamley had finished, Neil excused himself and dashed off.

He found the sergeant looking Sherlock over. "He's a fine animal. Very fine," he said, rubbing Sherlock's furry chest. The German shepherd put up a paw and rested it on the sergeant's arm. *It's almost as if he's saying, "take me home with you,"* thought Neil.

"I was very impressed with the way he tracked," continued the sergeant, as he scratched behind Sherlock's ears. Sherlock put his head on one side, his broad pink tongue lolling. He looked as if he were lapping up the praise.

"Yes. Isn't he smart?" said Neil brightly. "Don't you think he'd make a first-rate police dog?"

"I think he would," added Emily, who had just joined them.

"Definitely," Sergeant Moorhead said. Mr. Harding shot Neil a triumphant look and Neil gave him a thumbs-up sign behind the police sergeant's back. "I know Inspector Williams has already had a word with you about him. He'd like you to bring him to the training center for a full assessment — that is, if you're willing to part with him and allow the police to have him," he added.

"That's what I want most for him," Mr. Harding confirmed.

Inspector Williams and his colleagues stayed for a while to talk with the students of Meadowbank School and let them meet the dogs. Lots of people wanted to pet Sherlock and Oliver, too.

Neil went to get Jake to let him stretch his legs. A few pats and strokes would be just what he was looking for!

As he opened the gate to the courtyard, he spotted Mr. Harding talking to his father.

Suddenly, a shrill scream set all the dogs yapping. "A rat! I saw a rat in there," Mrs. Sharpe shouted, pointing toward the feed storeroom, where the door was slightly open. Neil guessed that Bev must have been getting things ready for the evening feeding.

Suddenly, Mr. Harding pointed toward the door. "Search," he ordered Sherlock.

As several people gathered around to watch the unfolding excitement, the young German shepherd nosed the door fully open and slipped inside. Then a sound came from inside the storeroom, a kind of high-pitched yelp.

"He's caught it," Mrs. Sharpe said excitedly.

Seconds later, Sherlock emerged with something brown and furry, held gently by the scruff of its neck, in his mouth. He dropped it at Mr. Harding's feet. It was very big for a rat. The small furry creature stood up, shook itself and gave a yap that was distinctly canine. It was Pepé.

"Bad dog!" said Carole. The tiny Chihuahua looked sheepish as she scooped him up. "I don't understand how he got out," said Carole worriedly. "It's never happened before."

"We'd better examine his pen before we put him back," Neil said.

At first glance, everything seemed fine. But when Neil actually felt the wire netting all over, he discovered that it was loose in the bottom right-hand corner, perhaps forced open by a particularly strong dog that had occupied the pen before him. No normal-sized dog could have squeezed through the tiny hole, but Pepé wasn't a normal-sized dog.

"So that's how he escaped," exclaimed Emily. "What a mischievous one!"

Pepé and his things were quickly transferred to a spare pen until the netting could be fixed later. Then Neil, Carole, and Bev went to inspect the damage in the feed storeroom.

Kate had just returned from her interview and looked surprised at all the attention Pepé was getting. "What's going on?" she wanted to know.

When Neil told her, he saw Kate looking thoughtfully at the sack of hamster food on the floor. It had neat little holes in the bottom and was leaking seeds and nuts. "I wonder . . ." she said. "I think I'll consult Mike about this, Neil."

"About what?" Neil asked, mystified.

"Just an idea of mine. I'll tell you when I find out if I'm right or wrong," she promised. Then she walked out and got on with her job again before Neil had a chance to ask her how her interview had gone. He set off after her, then spotted Mr. Harding and Sergeant Moorhead coming across the courtyard toward him.

"Is your father anywhere around?" the sergeant asked Neil.

"I think I saw him going over to the barn," Neil replied. Sherlock stuck his nose in Neil's hand. "Good boy," Neil said, giving him a pat. Sherlock thumped Neil's leg with his thick tail.

The sergeant's radio squawked and he started talking into it. Neil listened intently, knowing that he really shouldn't. "Yes . . . yes . . . Folly Lane . . . empty, you say? Right, I'm on my way."

He turned to Neil and Mr. Harding. "The car's turned up," he told them. His face was set in a fierce scowl. "Maybe this time I'll get the man who killed Jasper. Come on, Oliver."

As the sergeant rushed toward his car, Mr. Harding shouted, "Two dogs are better than one. I'll follow you," and made for his car.

Neil looked around for either of his parents, but they were not within earshot. "Let me come, too," Neil begged. Like the sergeant and Mr. Harding, he was just as anxious to see Jasper's killer brought to justice. Also, he longed to see Sherlock and Oliver involved in some real police action.

But Mr. Harding ended his hopes. "No," he said curtly. "I'm not taking you, and that's that. I'm in enough trouble with your parents already for all the danger I put you in after the antiques robberies. I want them to be able to trust me now, so we can all get along in the future. The dog business world is a small one, and I want to get a good reputation. I won't have that if I do something irresponsible and reckless, like taking you off on a hunt for a criminal!"

Neil stood his ground. "I'll take responsibility for myself, don't worry about that. I'll say I forced you to take me along with you. Dad knows how persuasive I can be."

"Look, I've got to go now or I'll never catch up with them. For the last time, Neil, you're not coming."

"Oh, yes, I am!" said Neil with determination, opening the passenger door. He saw his sister and yelled, "Em, I'm going back with Mr. Harding for a while . . ."

He would face the consequences later. For now, all Neil wanted was to be with Sherlock when Jasper's murderer was caught.

CHAPTER NINE

In the eerie half-light, as afternoon began to fade into evening, Neil and Mr. Harding drove along the twisting country road and climbed out of Compton toward the woods. Neil clutched the dashboard nervously as they rounded each bend, desperately trying to keep Sergeant Moorhead's police car in his sight. Behind him, Sherlock's eager panting tickled Neil's neck.

Then, turning a sweeping corner, they saw a longer stretch of road and found themselves the only car in the vicinity.

"We're here," said Mr. Harding.

"Where have they gone?" Neil asked anxiously. "We don't want to miss any of the action."

Folly Lane was a long, narrow road that skirted

Compton Woods and had high banks on either side, topped by thick hedges.

Mr. Harding slowed the car and crept slowly along the lane, just in case any police cars should speed toward them. The lane was dark, with trees that met overhead in many places, forming a tunnel. They crested a hill and then saw two parked police cars next to what Neil assumed was the abandoned stolen car.

Mr. Harding drew up behind them, stopped the car, and opened the back door for Sherlock to jump out.

Sherlock nudged Neil with his nose and Neil gave him a reassuring pat. Another big test for him might be just around the corner, and Neil didn't want the dog to be nervous.

"Neil," said Mr. Harding, "I really wish you'd stay in the car. I don't know what's going to happen next."

Neil nodded but began walking toward a shadowy path that led into the trees. "I'm OK. I won't do anything stupid."

Mr. Harding shrugged and set off after him, with Sherlock padding along between them.

Within a couple of minutes, they came upon Sergeant Moorhead, Oliver, and two other Compton police constables.

Neil nudged Mr. Harding. "Look at that," he said. "The sergeant is giving Oliver something to sniff."

Up ahead, in a small clearing, Sergeant Moorhead was holding something out to the dog. It looked like a jacket.

At the sound of Neil's voice, he swiveled around.

"What *are* you doing, bringing Neil with you?" the sergeant said angrily. "This could be dangerous!"

Neil tensed. "I wouldn't let him leave without me," he admitted. "There wasn't much he could do about it. So here I am."

"No, Neil, I can't expose you to any danger, you know that. Stay behind with Constable Grey, here," Sergeant Moorhead insisted, nodding toward one of his men.

Neil frowned. He didn't *want* to stay behind and miss seeing the dogs at work. Then he looked at the garment the policeman was holding out to Oliver. "Did you find that jacket in the car?" Neil asked.

"Yes. We think it belongs to the man we're after," said the sergeant.

"You believe he was working on his own, then?" Mr. Harding asked.

"Yes. That's what our information is," Sergeant Moorhead replied.

Oliver was still sniffing the jacket.

"Why don't you let Sherlock sniff it, too? You know how good he is at tracking," Neil said.

The sergeant looked up. "You're right. Two noses are better than one." Then he paused. "Though it is highly irregular. However, I know the inspector's keen to try Sherlock out."

Mr. Harding took the jacket and held it out for Sherlock. The German shepherd's tail started to wag. He whimpered and strained on his lead, sniffing keenly. Sherlock was obviously eager to set off after the scent. Oliver was agitated, too, but was sitting quietly, awaiting orders. Neil thought about the two dogs' different personalities. Sherlock seemed far more extroverted than Oliver, who was quieter and more reserved.

Sergeant Moorhead, the constable named Edwards, and Mr. Harding set off with the two dogs. Neil peered impatiently after them. It was growing darker every minute. He strained his eyes and saw that the group had halted in the center of the field. Suddenly, Neil heard the howl of a dog in trouble.

"Something's up!" cried Neil.

Constable Grey's eyes searched for the departed group among the trees. He shifted uncomfortably from one foot to the other.

Neil couldn't see what was wrong, but he *had* to find out. "Come on," he yelled and started to run into the trees.

Constable Grey shouted, "Hey! Come back," but raced after him instinctively.

When they caught up with the others, they found there was a stream flowing across the middle of the field. Recent rainstorms had swollen the waters until it was now more like a river. In places, the water had spread out and formed shallow ponds all along its banks.

"Does anyone know if there's any way around all this?" Sergeant Moorhead inquired.

"We could go farther into the woods, but it could be even more difficult to cross it there," said Neil quickly. He knew the woods very well because he walked Jake and Sam there so often on weekends. "The ground's steeper and rockier. We'd be scrambling over mossy stones and waterfalls. Both ways, we'd get very wet."

Sergeant Moorhead seemed surprised to see Neil so soon. "Not you again. I thought I told you to stay put?" He shook his head. "I haven't got time for this!" He quickly turned his attention back to the immediate problem.

"We might as well cross here," said Mr. Harding. "We should still be able to pick up the scent again on the other side." He and Sherlock carefully waded across. The water came up to the top of Sherlock's legs.

Neil splashed across after them, his sneakers managing to get enough grip on the streambed. He was scrambling up the bank on the other side when he heard a shout from behind and twisted around.

Sergeant Moorhead was standing in the middle of the stream, tugging forcibly on Oliver's leash. "Come on, Oliver!"

The German shepherd was pulling back, refusing to enter the water. He gave another forlorn howl like the one Neil had heard earlier.

"Let him off the leash," Neil suggested. "Maybe he wants to find his own way across."

Mr. Harding nodded.

The sergeant splashed back to Oliver and unclipped the leash. The German shepherd, whimpering miserably, backed even farther away from the water, sat down, and looked at the sergeant as if asking for help.

"Oliver, come on, it's all right," coaxed the sergeant. "What on earth's the matter with him?"

"Looks like he's scared of the water," Mr. Harding said. "I think you'll have to carry him."

The sergeant and Constable Edwards lifted the struggling, heavy German shepherd between them and carried him to the far side. Once he was put safely down on the muddy bank, he was a changed dog and seemed to recover his calm manner. But, during his troubles, he'd lost the scent and couldn't seem to pick it up again. By contrast, Sherlock was straining on his leash, his nose desperately sniffing the ground.

They set off again, this time following Sherlock alone. "Water's not a set part of a police dog's training routine," Mr. Harding informed everybody as they jogged along. "Sometimes you don't discover that a dog is afraid of water until a late stage. All dogs are natural swimmers, but, like people, some just don't like water."

"Can anything be done?" asked the sergeant breathlessly.

"Yes," Harding replied. "It can be fixed. I'm sure I could help him overcome his fear."

"We'll talk about it later," the sergeant said. "Let's get on with the search, while Sherlock still has the scent. He's the only one who can help us now."

Neil tagged along safely at the back, beside Constable Grey. The sergeant had insisted that Neil try not to get under their feet as they tracked the potentially dangerous criminal.

Within minutes, they came to the end of another field and had to scramble through wire fencing before they were in the woods once more. Sherlock had been in the woods before and was let loose. He ran ahead and plunged into the trees. As Oliver was still unfamiliar with the terrain, he remained on Sergeant Moorhead's leash, under more control.

It was much darker now, and all three policemen

produced flashlights and shone them on the path ahead. Even with the extra light, it was still difficult to avoid tree roots and loose stones as they climbed through the hilly woods. Mr. Harding told them how to get to a ruined house where he thought the man on the run might be heading. Harding had often walked Sherlock near here and had glimpsed it through the undergrowth.

Panting from the steepness and difficulty of the climb, they continued to make their way through the trees.

Suddenly, somewhere in the darkness way ahead of them, they heard an almost unearthly howling and barking that made the hairs along Neil's arms bristle.

"Sherlock's found something — or somebody," Harding said excitedly.

"Do you think Jasper's killer is still there?" asked Neil bitterly.

"He's either there, or he's been there recently," said Sergeant Moorhead. He looked down at his dogs. "Oliver's picked up the scent again. Look!" The lean, muscular German shepherd had his nose to the ground and occasionally stopped to sniff a branch that the man might have grasped as he hauled his way up the hill.

Sherlock howled again, much closer this time.

Constable Edwards raised his hand. "Listen," he said.

They all stopped moving. Then Neil heard, quite distinctly, a man's voice swearing at Sherlock. Sherlock yelped and they heard something thudding in the undergrowth very close by. It sounded like somebody was throwing rocks at the dog. Neil blazed with anger.

"Neil, stay here with Constable Grey," the sergeant barked. The constable looked at Neil somewhat resentfully. "Harding, Edwards, follow me."

Neil pretended he hadn't heard and shot forward with the others. Pushing their way through thick, prickly bushes, they found themselves at a ruined one-story cottage. The thief had certainly chosen a good hiding place. Neil didn't think many people would have bothered to push their way through all those thorns just to explore.

A tree grew over the crumbling walls, forming a makeshift roof. Sherlock was barking at a hole in a wall where a window had been. Constable Edwards stepped in front of Neil and swung his flashlight toward the black cavity.

There, illuminated in the blinding beam, was the face of a man of about thirty. He was unshaven and had a black wool hat pulled down as far as his eyebrows.

"Call that dog off," he shouted desperately.

Neil could see the expression on Sergeant Moorhead's face. He had never, *ever* seen a man look so angry. At that moment, Neil realized how much the policeman had wanted to catch the man who killed Jasper.

But he still had to be apprehended.

The police acted swiftly as a professional unit.

Mr. Harding grabbed Sherlock's collar and Neil quickly took cover behind the huge, solid trunk of a beech tree nearby.

"Give up!" Sergeant Moorhead ordered toward the cottage. "You can't get away now."

The man shouted defiantly and refused to emerge.

"Then we're coming in!" yelled the sergeant, his flashlight beam shining on the crumbling window. All three officers moved forward, homing in on different entrances to the building.

Neil saw the man's face disappear inside. Then there was a clatter of loose stones and the man appeared again, on what was left of the roof. From there, he leaped onto an overhanging branch and began to swing along it, hand over hand.

"Grab him!" Sergeant Moorhead yelled down to Oliver.

Neil drew a sharp intake of breath when he saw Sherlock, not Oliver, respond first with an enormous bound toward the ruined building. Jumping up, Sherlock gripped the man's left ankle in his fierce jaws.

The man yelled in pain and kicked out at the dog wildly, but the German shepherd's weight dragged the man from his branch. He landed with a thump on the stony ground and rolled over. Immediately, he was jumped on by the two constables. Constable Edwards held the man's arms behind his back while Constable Grey clipped some handcuffs on to finally restrain him. Only then was Sherlock given the order by Mr. Harding to release his grip on the man's ankle.

"Well done, Sherlock, good dog," said Sergeant Moorhead, ruffling his fur vigorously. Sherlock tilted his head, then butted the sergeant's head with his nose and licked it. *They like each other,* thought Neil. Oliver, too, was given a pat so that he wouldn't feel left out, but there was no doubt in anyone's mind that all the glory belonged to Sherlock.

The constable frisked the burglar. Zipped into the inside pocket of his jacket they found a plastic bag containing the stolen watches and jewelry.

"Thanks for lending us Sherlock," the sergeant told Mr. Harding. "He really has been an asset on this job. I've known dogs who've graduated from dog training college who wouldn't have had the intelligence to size up the situation and bring that man down from the tree. All credit to you, Harding. And to Sherlock, of course." He bent down and ruffled the dog's neck fur.

Neil watched as the sergeant stroked and patted Sherlock again. He seemed very pleased. Neil felt sure they would easily bond — if only they got the chance. He was so proud of Sherlock and couldn't help smiling when he saw the beaming face of an equally proud Mr. Harding.

Sergeant Moorhead stood up and moved in front of the burglar, whose arms were gripped on each side by a sturdy constable. "As for you," he said to the quaking man, who hung his head, "you deserve to go to prison for what you did to my dog! And I hope you do."

CHAPTER TEN

"**A**nd just where have you been?" Bob Parker thundered, back at King Street, as Neil nervously opened the passenger door of Mr. Harding's car. "You told Emily you were going home with Mr. Harding and you'd be back *soon*. That was more than two hours ago!"

Neil's dad turned to Harding, who was letting Sherlock out of the car. "We phoned several times and your wife said you weren't back yet. We've been really worried. What's been going on?"

"Allow me to explain —" began Mr. Harding, but Neil broke in.

"Sorry, Dad," he said. "Sergeant Moorhead got a message to say they'd found the car that was driven by the man who killed Jasper. He took Oliver to see if there was any scent for him to follow and Mr. Harding decided to follow him in case Sherlock could help out."

"How dare you take my son with you!" Bob boomed, facing Mr. Harding. "It could have been really dangerous!"

"Please, Dad. It wasn't Mr. Harding's fault, it was mine. I insisted he take me with him. I got in the car and wouldn't get out. He didn't have any choice," Neil admitted.

"You *lied* to Emily, too," Bob continued angrily. "I'm sure you could have stopped him from getting into your car, James," he accused Harding.

Mr. Harding shrugged and sighed. "Sorry, Bob, but once your son gets an idea in his head, there's nothing you can do with him," he said.

"*Tell me about it*," Neil's father replied grimly. "But I don't expect a responsible adult to encourage him and —"

"He didn't encourage me. Oh, Dad, it was great! Sherlock caught the burglar and I was never in any danger because the police made me stay behind a tree. Poor old Oliver, though. He really let himself down. He wouldn't cross the stream. It turns out he's afraid of water. So what we did was —"

Bob Parker threw up his hands. "I give up!" He sighed heavily. "Please promise me you'll never do anything foolhardy like that again," he snapped.

"Yes, Dad. Of course, Dad. When we got to the woods, we heard Sherlock howling like a wolf. It was amazing! So we . . ." As Neil continued eagerly describing the happiness of the last two hours, they gradually moved toward the house, where Carole, Emily, and Sarah were standing in the doorway, waiting to hear what had happened.

At the end of Neil's story, Sherlock was heavily patted and praised and even given a dog treat by Carole — a rare honor indeed! "He really is a wonderful dog," she said. "The way he pulled that burglar out of the tree! I'm really, really glad that they've got the man who killed Jasper at last. Poor Sergeant Moorhead . . ."

They all got quiet for a moment, thinking of Jasper. Then Carole said, "Tell me, James, what do you plan to do to get Oliver over his phobia?"

"Well, if the police let me, I plan to introduce him to water gradually. Something like a small paddling pool at first," Harding explained. "I'd let him see Jessie playing in it, so he can see that water can be fun. It's my theory that perhaps something happened to him when he was a puppy. Maybe he was forced to have a bath or fell in a pond, and it was an unpleasant, scary experience for him. Who knows? He's a good dog. I'm sure it would be worth it."

"If you can't do it, who can?" said Neil. "Look how well you've trained Sherlock and Jessie!"

Both Carole and Bob nodded their approval.

Mom's getting to like him at last! Neil thought cheerfully.

Neil got up late the next morning, after a night full of dreams involving Sherlock chasing burglars through the woods. By the time he had eaten his breakfast and walked Sam and Jake, Mike Turner had arrived to start his regular Saturday morning clinic. Just as Neil was crossing the courtyard to have a word with Mike, Kate called him over. She was looking happier than she had for a long time.

"Neil, Neil . . . listen to this!" she said, waving a sheet of paper.

Oh, no, he thought, *she's been offered the SPCA job!* "Did you get it, then?" he asked her.

Kate frowned. "Get what? Oh, you mean the job. I'll tell you about that in a minute. No, these are Pepé's allergy test results. I had a hunch that he might be allergic to nuts because there was some in the hamster food. Lots of people have nut allergies, so I thought, why not dogs? I mentioned it to Mike and he took samples from Pepé yesterday and got his allergy specialist friend to rush the analysis through."

"I thought Mike said he had to wait till Pepé's owner got back?" Neil asked.

"True, but he realized that if I was right, Pepé's owner should be told right away," Kate explained.

"Imagine if she had a welcome home party and Pepé got his nose in a bowl of peanuts and started scarfing them up and had another attack? These things are best identified as soon as possible. Anyway, I was right! There's a certain type of mold that can grow on raw peanuts, and *that's* what he's allergic to."

"Will he be OK?"

"He'll be fine — as long as he keeps away from them. Mike's got a leaflet on allergies for us to give to Pepé's owner."

Bev had joined them while they were talking. "You're a genius, Kate," she said. "I'd never have thought of the peanut connection." Kate smiled a glowing smile and Bev headed on toward the kennel blocks.

"Now, tell me how the interview went," Neil said nervously, once they were alone again. He didn't know how much Kate had already told the others.

Kate blushed. "OK, I think."

Oh, great, thought Neil. "So that means, if they offer you the job, you'll go?" he asked. But the answer was quite the opposite of the one he was expecting.

"No," said Kate.

"What do you mean, no?" Neil asked. He couldn't believe what he was hearing.

"Exactly that. Whether they offer it to me or not, I'm not leaving King Street Kennels." Kate folded her arms and looked at him, her lips twitching slightly.

Neil stared at her. "Why not?" he asked her.

"It's all your fault," she told him. "Remember that day you and Emily were trying to persuade me to stay?"

"Yes," Neil said. How could he forget? He'd seldom felt like such a failure.

"That's when I realized I didn't want another kennel assistant doing my job. I love working here, with you and the dogs. I can't imagine being this happy anywhere else."

Wow, thought Neil happily. All this time, he'd been positive that Kate had turned deaf ears to what he and Em had said that day. But she hadn't. She'd actually listened and thought about it. *What a great result!*

"It was stupid of me to feel I wasn't needed," Kate continued. "Just because you'd taken on Bev as well. There's more than enough work for the two of us. And I *like* Bev. We're really good friends now. So I hope you don't mind putting up with me for a while longer. . . ." Kate's eyes danced.

Neil let his happy grin show how he felt.

There was a line of people with their dogs waiting to see Mike. Neil popped his head in and asked for the leaflet about allergies because he wanted to research the facts. He was becoming so interested in dogs' health that, not for the first time, he wondered if he might end up training to be a vet himself.

He sat on the wall by the barn and was reading up on allergy symptoms when he saw a police car coming down the driveway. Sergeant Moorhead was at the wheel. Neil ran to greet him. The sergeant let Oliver out of the back and the German shepherd ran up to Neil, wagging his tail.

"Hello, Oliver," Neil said, stroking the dog's head. "Hi, Sergeant Moorhead."

"Oh, I see. Dogs first, humans second," the sergeant joked.

Neil gave an embarrassed grin.

"Don't worry, I agree with you." Sergeant Moorhead laughed. "Now, is Mr. Harding here, by any chance? When I phoned him earlier, he said he was dropping into King Street Kennels about noon."

"I haven't seen him," Neil replied with a frown. He wondered why his parents hadn't told him. Unless, of course, Mr. Harding's visit was an unofficial one and they didn't know.

The sound of a car startled them both. It was Mr. Harding and his wife, Barbara. He beeped his horn and Jessie and Sherlock barked a greeting from the backseat.

Neil was soon bending down to greet both dogs with an affectionate hug.

They all walked over to the kitchen, where Neil knew his father was reading his newspaper. "Oh, hello," he said, getting up from the table. "I wasn't expecting visitors. . . ."

The large kitchen was suddenly full of dogs, as two German shepherds mingled with two Border collies and one Airedale cross. Neil smiled happily as he was jostled by warm, hairy bodies and thumped by wagging tails. Hearing the commotion, Carole, Emily, and Sarah all crowded into the kitchen, too, to find out what was happening. It felt like there was a party going on.

"I came to thank you all for your help," announced Sergeant Moorhead. "And to tell you that the man we caught has been formally charged with committing burglary. But that's not all," Sergeant Moorhead said. "The SPCA is going to carry out its own private prosecution because of his deliberate cruelty to Jasper."

"That's really good news," exclaimed Bob.

Jessie had found her way to Carole's side. Carole stroked her and held on to her collar so that there would be one less wandering dog for everybody to trip over. Jake had found Jessie, whom he adored, and was snuggled up next to her, lying across Barbara Harding's foot.

"I spoke to Inspector Williams this morning," the sergeant told Mr. Harding. "He wants to know if you could bring Sherlock over to the training school in Padsham on Tuesday, so he can try him out."

"Sure," responded Harding.

"What about Oliver?" asked Neil.

"Well, I've recommended to the inspector that,

since Mr. Harding has special skills with dogs, he should be officially appointed to help finish his training and see if he can cure him of his water aversion. What do you say, Mr. Harding?"

"If he makes the offer, I'll only be too happy to accept," said Mr. Harding. "My first official customer! I think Oliver and I could work well together. What do you say, boy?"

Mr. Harding stroked the ears of the tall, strong German shepherd and Oliver leaned against Mr. Harding's legs and licked his hand. Neil could see that the dog trusted and accepted Mr. Harding. That was the first hurdle overcome.

Neil spoke the burning question that was on everybody's minds. "But nobody knows how long Oliver's special training will take, Sergeant. And you need another dog fairly soon. What are the chances of you being allowed to have Sherlock?"

The policeman smiled. "Extremely good, I should think," he replied. "He'll need to complete another three-week police dog training course, where I'm sure he'll do well — especially after the excellent start Mr. Harding's given him. But there's another important factor to take into consideration, too . . ." He paused and looked around at everyone.

Emily couldn't wait for him to continue. "What's that?" she prompted eagerly.

The sergeant laughed. "I think we've taken to one another!" he said, scratching Sherlock's head. The

German shepherd's amber eyes glowed as he looked
up at the sergeant. Neil knew love between dog and
man when he saw it. He felt sure that the two were
well on their way to becoming inseparable as the
sergeant and Jasper had once been.

"Awesome!" yelled Neil.

Everybody laughed.

"Well done, Sherlock," Neil said, giving the dog a
big pat. "Jasper would be really proud of you."

Sherlock barked his agreement.